FACING
THE DEMON
HEADMASTER

The most hypnotic villain of all . . .

Get ready for adventure and intrigue.

Prepare to fall under his spell.

Do not try to resist . . .

Are you ready to meet the Demon Headmaster? Here's a taste of what's to come . . .

Lloyd couldn't take his eyes off the glittering figure on the stage. As the first song came to an end, DJ Pardoman stopped moving and faced into the crowded club. This time, his face looked exactly like Brad Pitt's.

'So—that was this week's Number One,' he said. 'What next?' His voice was very distinctive. Deep and melodious, with a raw, harsh edge to it.

People started to roar out the names of songs and bands, and he stood and listened. Or so it seemed. His face was still shifting, but his head was tilted attentively and his whole body was still.

The moment the roar began to fade, he held up both hands. 'Here we go, then!'

Music came flooding out of the speakers and he started prancing along the back of the stage again. He had a baby's face now—bigger than any real baby's, but with the same, smooth, bald head and the same sleepy grin.

How did he do it? Was he wearing some kind of mask? Lloyd glanced round to catch Dinah's attention, but she didn't see him. She was standing completely still, gazing at the stage.

Ingrid came bouncing up, dancing vigorously. 'Isn't he wonderful?' she yelled.

'How d'you think it's done?' Lloyd shouted.

Ingrid gave him a wise look. 'Technology,' she said. And she danced away again.

After the next song, DJ Pardoman stopped dancing

and waved a hand. As if by magic, a map of the whole country appeared behind him, shimmering against the wall. He looked down from the stage—with the face of a wrinkled old woman—and drawled a question.

'Where's—Purple?'

Immediately, people began to call out answers.

'Manchester!'

'Birmingham!'

'Swansea!'

'Glasgow!'

'Newcastle!'

As they called, he clicked his fingers and purple dots began to blossom all over the map. Not just one at a time, but in twos and threes—and more. There were six in Liverpool. Three in Cardiff. A couple of dozen in and around London. Lloyd tried to keep a count, but when it went over a hundred he lost track of the number.

'And—this week,' drawled DJ Pardoman—out of the Prime Minister's mouth—'this week we have—Inverness! Give them a welcome!'

The map beside him changed into the picture of a city viewed from the air. The camera homed in, swooping over rooftops and zooming in on a little cluster of streets near the edge of the city. Hundreds of young people—thousands of them—were crowding round a big building on the far side of a car park.

PURPLE!!! screamed the sign over the gleaming silver shutter.

'PURPLE!!!' yelled all the voices around Dinah.

OXFORD
UNIVERSITY PRESS

Great Clarendon Street, Oxford OX2 6DP
Oxford University Press is a department of the University of Oxford.
It furthers the University's objective of excellence in research, scholarship,
and education by publishing worldwide. Oxford is a registered trade mark
of Oxford University Press in the UK and in certain other countries

British Library Cataloguing in Publication Data

Data available

ISBN: 978-0-19-276372-3

1 3 5 7 9 10 8 6 4 2

Printed in India by Replika Press Pvt. Ltd.

Paper used in the production of this book is a natural,
recyclable product made from wood grown in sustainable forests.
The manufacturing process conforms to the environmental
regulations of the country of origin.

FACING THE DEMON HEADMASTER

GILLIAN CROSS

OXFORD
UNIVERSITY PRESS

CONTENTS

1

PURPLE

'Ellie's completely changed since she started going to Purple!' Mandy said breathlessly. 'She says it's the most fantastic club there's ever been, and the DJ's brilliant! She wants to take us next time!'

All six members of SPLAT were sitting in Ian's lounge, drinking milkshakes. Mandy looked round at them, her face pink and eager.

'Well?' she said. 'Shall we go?'

How can a club be that great? thought Dinah. She didn't know Mandy's cousin Ellie, but she knew Mandy very well. And it took a lot to get her so excited. Was it really worth going to this Purple thing—whatever it was? Dinah glanced at the other four, to see what they were thinking.

Lloyd and Harvey—her two adopted brothers—had quite different expressions. Harvey was beaming, but Lloyd looked cautious. He wouldn't give a lead until he knew what everyone thought.

Ingrid was grinning and blowing bubbles down her straw. 'Let's make it a SPLAT outing! On Wednesday. That's the next Under Eighteens night, isn't it?'

Lloyd nodded, but he was still being cautious. He looked at Ian. 'What do you think?'

Ian leaned back in his chair, stretching out his long legs. 'I'm not *desperately* keen,' he drawled. 'But I'll go along with the rest of you, of course, if that's what we're doing.'

Lloyd was counting heads. 'We've got three in favour—Mandy and Harvey and Ingrid—and two of us who aren't sure. What about you, Di? Fancy a visit to Purple?'

Dinah frowned. 'I don't know anything about it. What's it like? Are all the walls purple, or something?'

'Of course not!' Ingrid said scornfully.

'So why is it called Purple?' said Dinah.

Shut up! Lloyd and Harvey both pulled faces at Dinah. *Don't be embarrassing!* But once Dinah started asking questions about something, she went on until she understood.

'Do you have to wear purple to get in?' she said.

Lloyd sighed and Harvey put his hands over his face.

'Where do you *live*? In a box?' Ingrid rolled her eyes up at the ceiling. 'Purple's been all over the television for weeks. In every magazine. Plastered across the newspapers. There are clubs opening up everywhere.'

Dinah shrugged. 'Well, I've been busy. There's lots of new research coming out about the socio-biology of feelings and facial expression—'

All the others groaned, and Lloyd threw a cushion at her to make her shut up.

'Who cares about science?' Ingrid growled. Mandy reached over and patted her shoulder. 'Calm down,

Ing. You can't expect a genius like Di to be interested in clubs.'

'Don't see why not,' Ingrid muttered. 'I thought science was about the real world. Purple's part of that. We've got to know about it!'

'She's right, Di.' Lloyd nodded, making up his mind. 'I vote for checking it out—and that makes four in favour. We'll have a SPLAT outing on Wednesday.'

'Fine,' said Dinah.

She wasn't going to argue any more now they'd voted. She might not care much about clubs, but SPLAT meant a lot to her. The Society for the Protection of our Lives Against Them. They were her best friends in the world and the six of them had been through a lot together. Battling against the sinister Headmaster and his plans to control the world had led them into all kinds of problems and dangers and they knew they could rely on one another.

They were SPLAT and they stuck together.

'What time do we leave on Wednesday?' she said.

Mandy beamed. 'It starts at half past seven. But we'll need to be there just after six to get in. Ellie said there was a massive queue last week.'

'OK,' Lloyd said. 'We'll meet at our house, and get the five forty-five bus.'

'Fine.' Ingrid sucked up the last drops of her milkshake. 'I'll be round straight after school!'

'Me too,' said Mandy. 'As soon as I've been home to pick up my stuff.'

'Why do you need to come so early?' Dinah was mystified.

Mandy laughed. 'We've got to get you dressed right. And Lloyd and Harvey might need a bit of advice too.'

'You don't need to worry about us,' Lloyd said stiffly. 'We know how to dress ourselves. Don't we, H?'

Harvey hesitated.

'Of course you do,' Mandy said gently. 'But it's a bit different with Purple.'

'It's only a club!' Lloyd was getting annoyed. 'I'm perfectly capable of choosing what to wear.'

On Wednesday, Mandy and Ingrid turned up at quarter past four, both with bulging carrier bags. Lloyd and Harvey stared at them.

'You can't wear that many clothes!' Harvey said.

'Got to have something to choose from,' said Ingrid. 'Come on, Di.'

Lloyd shook his head. 'Why has it got to be so complicated? I know exactly what I'm going to wear. And it'll only take me ten minutes to change.'

Secretly, Dinah agreed with him. But she knew better than to argue with Ingrid. And whatever Ingrid and Mandy were going to do, it couldn't be that terrible. It was only clothes, after all. It couldn't really matter what she wore.

It was almost an hour before Ingrid and Mandy were

satisfied with how Dinah looked. By the time the three of them finally came rattling downstairs, it was after half past five and Lloyd and Harvey were just opening the front door to Ian.

Lloyd turned round and stared at Dinah. 'What *are* you wearing?'

'Purple chic!' Dinah said cheerfully.

She and Mandy and Ingrid spun round to show off their outfits.

Their hair was loose and they had a lot of make-up on. Even Dinah, who never used anything like that, was wearing lipstick and blusher and nail varnish. And they all had beads round their necks and armfuls of bangles. That was what had taken all the time to choose and arrange. The actual clothes had been easy.

They were wearing the oldest things they could lay their hands on.

Dinah had found a pair of ancient, frayed jeans and borrowed a worn-out top from Mandy. Her trainers were grubby and starting to split—but they'd been smartened up with a new pair of fluorescent laces.

'This is how you ought to be dressed, Lloyd,' Ingrid said triumphantly. 'You and Harvey have got your best things on—and they're going to get really messy.'

Lloyd frowned. 'Why should they?'

Mandy and Ingrid looked at each other and giggled. Mandy took a bunch of bananas out of her little backpack and waved them under his nose.

'*It's bananas this week*,' she said. 'That's what Ellie told me. *Make sure you've got some bananas.*'

Ingrid giggled again at Lloyd's baffled expression. 'Didn't you see that article in *Lipstick* last week? People take stuff to Purple—'

'—something different every week—' Mandy said. 'And if you haven't got the right thing—'

'—it's *really terrible*!' Ingrid pulled out a bunch of bananas too.

Ian was still in the doorway. He was in old clothes too, with a flashy coloured belt to hold up his jeans. Suddenly he produced some bananas from behind his back.

'Purple chic for ever!' he said. 'Save money on clothes and spend it at the supermarket!'

Harvey was gazing at him wide-eyed. 'Have you been reading *Lipstick* too?'

'Of course not!' Ian spluttered indignantly. 'Mandy told me.'

'Why didn't she tell us then?' Lloyd growled.

Ingrid opened her eyes wide. 'But *you* said you knew all *about* Purple,' she murmured innocently.

Dinah broke in quickly before an argument could start. 'So—do we need bananas too?'

'If you can get them,' Mandy said.

Lloyd was already charging into the kitchen. 'Got any bananas, Mum?'

Mrs Hunter lifted a bunch out of the fruit bowl. 'Do you want one?'

Lloyd glanced over his shoulder at Harvey and Dinah. Then he looked back at the bananas. 'Can I have them all?'

'All?' Mrs Hunter raised her eyebrows. 'I was going to make a banoffi pie.'

Harvey followed Lloyd into the kitchen. '*Please!*' he said. 'It's really important. We need bananas to take to Purple.'

'Sounds crazy to me,' Mrs Hunter said. Then she grinned. 'But I don't want you to be left out. Here you are.' She held out the bunch of bananas. 'And mind you don't miss the bus home.'

'We won't. Thanks, Mum. You're brilliant!' Lloyd grabbed the bananas and raced out into the hall. 'Let's go!' he said.

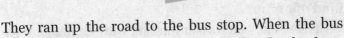

They ran up the road to the bus stop. When the bus arrived, Mandy's cousin Ellie was standing by the door, watching out for them.

She looked them up and down as they scrambled on, but it was impossible to tell what she was thinking. Her face was dead white and expressionless and she was wearing dark purple lipstick and a lot of black eye make-up. Dinah had never seen anyone in such old, ragged clothes or so much jewellery. She had a ring on every finger—and a purple phone clipped to her belt.

'Did you remember what I told you?' Ellie muttered to Mandy. Her mouth hardly moved when she spoke.

Mandy nodded eagerly and opened the top of her little backpack. 'It's OK. We've all got some.'

'Even *him*?' Ellie jerked her head at Lloyd.

'Yes!' Lloyd said crossly. He sat down and turned his back on her.

Dinah could see he was annoyed. 'It'll be OK,' she muttered, sitting down beside him. 'We don't have to go again if we don't like it.'

'I'm fine,' Lloyd said quickly.

Have it your own way. Dinah sat back and looked round the bus. There were quite a few people she knew—and lots of strangers too. And they were all wearing make-up and old clothes dressed up with glitter and belts and badges. A couple of other people had super-white faces and dark eyes, like Ellie. Was that a coincidence? Or were they some kind of group?

The whole bus was simmering with excitement. No one was talking much about Purple, but every now and again people would slide bunches of bananas out of their backpacks, showing just an inch or two of stalk. Dinah saw the question in their eyes. *Is this the right thing?* It was easy to see who'd got it wrong. One or two people went pale and looked away.

'When the bus stops, they'll be straight into the supermarket,' Ellie muttered. 'You watch.'

The bus pulled up by the big supermarket at the edge of town. The three boys without bananas jumped up—looking red-faced and sheepish—and bolted out of the bus, racing towards the supermarket while people on the bus booed and jeered.

There were a couple of dozen teenagers ahead of them, already pushing their way into the supermarket in front of the other shoppers. Dinah could see people glaring at them and muttering together.

'They're in for some hassle,' Ellie said coolly. 'Last week it was flour, and the clubbers bought up the lot. The regular shoppers went mad.'

Harvey frowned. 'But what's it all about? Why do we *need* bananas?'

'You'll find out,' Ellie said. She stood up and led them off the bus. Once they were all off, she set out quickly, trying to get ahead of everyone else.

They went down one side of the supermarket. Behind it was a huge car park, crammed with people. They were talking and laughing, and all of them were trying to edge closer to the long, low building on the far side.

There was no mistaking what it was. Big cut-out letters stood up on top, flashing as they spelt out the name. PURPLE!!! Below that, the whole front of the club was covered by a silver shutter that glittered and sparkled, in a constantly changing pattern.

Ingrid stared unhappily at the crowd. 'We'll never get in.'

'Of course we will,' Ellie said. 'Just follow me.' Without altering her deadpan expression, she put her head down and started to wriggle her way through the crowd.

Mandy grabbed Ingrid's hand. 'Come on! We've got to keep up with her.'

They all squeezed after Ellie, in single file, weaving their way along the corridor she opened up for them.

One or two people shouted at them, but Ellie ignored that and ploughed on, with her head down. She didn't stop until they were within fifteen metres of the big silver shutter.

'That should do,' she said.

Harvey looked nervously over his shoulder at the people behind. 'What about them? When the door opens, they'll all start pushing. We'll be squashed!'

'Don't be stupid,' Ellie said coldly. 'D'you think this is some small town club? They've got that sorted.' Mandy patted Harvey's hand. 'Don't worry. Ellie knows what she's doing. Just have your money ready.'

It seemed like a long wait. But, just as Dinah was ready to give up and go home, everyone in the crowd suddenly began to chant.

'TEN! NINE! EIGHT! SEVEN! SIX! FIVE! . . . '

'Ready?' Ellie said.

' . . . FOUR! THREE! TWO! ONE!—ZERO!!!' roared the crowd.

Precisely on time, the huge silver shutter began to slide up, into the thickness of the wall above. Behind it was a row of gleaming arches separated by stout silver pillars. There were twenty or thirty arches, running across the front of the building, and in front of each pillar stood a huge man dressed in a purple tracksuit.

'See the heavies?' Ellie said. 'They won't let anyone squash you, Harvey.'

Beyond the arches, there was a vast, dark space. Dinah saw lights flashing and heard music pounding from a stage in the far corner. The crowd surged forward, towards the arches, and she braced herself, ready to be pushed by the people behind.

But there was hardly any pushing. People went through the arches in an orderly, steady fashion. Dinah soon found out why.

A little way ahead of her, a boy lost patience and started to shove at the people in front. They let him through—but as he walked under an arch, the heavies on each side of it stepped forward and lifted him roughly off his feet.

He yelled furiously, but the heavies didn't react. With blank, uncaring faces, they hoisted him into the air and threw him, hard, towards the crowd. Dozens of hands grabbed him and he was passed back, from one group to another, until he was on the far side of the car park.

'That fixed him!' Ellie said. 'He won't get in this evening.'

She was at the front now, and she stepped forward into an arch. The pillar had two openings in it and she slid her money into the smaller one. Then she pushed her hand into the other for a second—and she was through.

'You next, Ing,' Mandy said. 'Just do the same as Ellie.'

Ingrid dropped her money in, put a hand into the other opening—and giggled. 'It tickles!'

When she took the hand out again there was a luminous entrance stamp on the back of it. A purple star that rippled and shifted as she moved her fingers.

Dinah followed her. Once she was through the arch, she headed for the far corner, where the music was being played, but Ellie caught at her sleeve.

'Not there!' she said. 'The main show's over here.'

Dinah didn't like being pulled about, but she let Ellie guide her, and the others followed. As they swung round, a huge voice boomed over their heads.

'You people outside are UNlucky today. Stand clear of the shutter.'

There were yells of disappointment from the people who hadn't made it inside. The huge silver shutter began to slide down again, cutting out all the light from the car park. For a split second the lights inside the club went out too and the music stopped.

There was an instant of complete darkness and silence.

Then, into the silence, a deep voice spoke. A musical, growling whisper, amplified to fill the whole space around them.

'So now—it's the gooooood music . . . '

Everyone roared and the lights went up on a different stage, running all down one side of the club. As the music started, a glittering shape began to move along the back of the stage, half walking and half dancing. His moving hands darted left and right, pointing commandingly at the great bank of equipment in front of him, and his face stared out at the crowd.

He looks like Elvis, Dinah thought, startled.

But the moment she thought it—the face on the stage changed.

20

It was one of the weirdest, most unsettling things she'd ever seen. One moment she was gazing at an Elvis lookalike—next moment it was an older man, with bright, piercing eyes and a wry smile. And then—

Ingrid screeched with laughter. 'That's Madonna!'

The prancing, dancing figure stayed the same, but the face kept shifting unpredictably. Dinah looked round at Ellie.

'Who *is* he?' she said.

But even before Ellie replied, she knew the answer. Everyone was saying the name, all over the club.

'It's DJ Pardoman!'

LOOK INTO MY EYES

2

DJ PARDOMAN

Lloyd couldn't take his eyes off the glittering figure on the stage. As the first song came to an end, DJ Pardoman stopped moving and faced into the crowded club. This time, his face looked exactly like Brad Pitt's.

'So—that was this week's Number One,' he said. 'What next?' His voice was very distinctive. Deep and melodious, with a raw, harsh edge to it.

People started to roar out the names of songs and bands, and he stood and listened. Or so it seemed. His face was still shifting, but his head was tilted attentively and his whole body was still.

The moment the roar began to fade, he held up both hands. 'Here we go, then!'

Music came flooding out of the speakers and he started prancing along the back of the stage again. He had a baby's face now—bigger than any real baby's, but with the same, smooth, bald head and the same sleepy grin.

How did he do it? Was he wearing some kind of mask? Lloyd glanced round to catch Dinah's attention, but she didn't see him. She was standing completely still, gazing at the stage.

Ingrid came bouncing up, dancing vigorously. 'Isn't he wonderful?' she yelled.

'How d'you think it's done?' Lloyd shouted.

Ingrid gave him a wise look. 'Technology,' she said. And she danced away again.

After the next song, DJ Pardoman stopped dancing and waved a hand. As if by magic, a map of the whole country appeared behind him, shimmering against the wall. He looked down from the stage—with the face of a wrinkled old woman—and drawled a question.

'Where's—Purple?'

Immediately, people began to call out answers.

'Manchester!'

'Birmingham!'

'Swansea!'

'Glasgow!'

'Newcastle!'

As they called, he clicked his fingers and purple dots began to blossom all over the map. Not just one at a time, but in twos and threes—and more. There were six in Liverpool. Three in Cardiff. A couple of dozen in and around London. Lloyd tried to keep a count, but when it went over a hundred he lost track of the number.

'And—this week,' drawled DJ Pardoman—out of the Prime Minister's mouth—'this week we have— Inverness! Give them a welcome!'

The map beside him changed into the picture of a city viewed from the air. The camera homed in, swooping over rooftops and zooming in on a little cluster of streets near the edge of the city. Hundreds of young people—thousands of them—were crowding round a big building on the far side of a car park.

PURPLE!!! screamed the sign over the gleaming silver shutter.

'PURPLE!!!' yelled all the voices around Dinah.

As they screamed, a big limousine appeared in the car park on the screen. It edged its way through the crowd until it reached the front of the club. Half a dozen people climbed out—men in suits and heavies dressed in purple—but no one paid any attention to them. Everyone was gazing at the glittering figure who jumped out of the car—and leapt straight on to its roof. He raised both arms above his head and then began dancing and pointing in a way that Lloyd recognized straight away.

The people round him stamped and yelled. 'DJP! DJP!'

'That's me all right!' DJ Pardoman called from the stage. 'I'm up in Inverness—and I'm here too! I'm there and I'm here—and I'm everywhere!'

And then the picture had vanished, and they were into the next song.

After that break, the music went on without stopping until it was almost ten o'clock.

At four minutes to ten, DJ Pardoman suddenly held up a hand.

'We're going into the last track,' he drawled, looking at them with Mickey Mouse's face. 'After that—it's the end.'

Lloyd expected the audience to groan, but nobody

did. Everyone cheered, and there was a tremendous buzz of excitement. The last song was loud and fast, with an insistent beat, and people were dancing wildly, watching the doors. Waiting for something.

As the song drew to a close, DJ Pardoman yelled, 'It's OVER!'

Then he vanished. All the lights went out and the silver shutter began to rise. Lloyd heard a sudden gasp and a burst of laughter from the people who were near enough to see outside.

Then he was swept forward in a rush down the length of the club. He found himself running through an arch and out into the car park. And ahead of him was a sight that didn't make sense.

People were launching themselves forward and sliding the length of the car park. They slithered from one end to another, as though the asphalt surface had suddenly been turned into a vast ice rink.

But ice rinks were white. Not black.

For a second, Lloyd was baffled. Then he got it—and he laughed out loud, like the people ahead of him.

It wasn't ice out there—it was *banana skins*!

Hundreds and hundreds of people had thrown down their bananas and the whole car park was covered with the skins. Hundreds of pairs of sliding feet had already battered them into blackness.

Ellie was halfway across the car park, swooping elegantly forward as though she'd spent her whole life sliding on banana skins.

'YES!' Ingrid yelled. She pulled out her bananas

and flung them to the ground. Then she threw herself forward recklessly. She staggered for a moment and then found her balance and zoomed forward.

'Let me have a go!' Harvey shouted.

He ran forward eagerly, ready to slide. But before he could get going, three girls stepped out of the crowd and grabbed him roughly.

'Bananas!' they said.

Their faces were as white as Ellie's and they were utterly without expression. The blankness was more frightening than bared teeth and Harvey began to shiver.

'Di!' Lloyd looked round for her. 'Have you got our bananas?'

Dinah pulled the bunch out of her backpack and broke off a couple for Harvey. The three girls gave a curt nod and stepped back into the crowd. Harvey threw the bananas and then launched himself forward, sliding fifty metres before he pitched over and landed in a heap of banana mush.

'Let's go!' Lloyd said excitedly. He snatched two bananas out of Dinah's hand, waved them in the air, to prove that he had them, and threw them on to the ground. Taking a run, he planted his feet on the skins and SLI-I-I-I-ID.

It was Mandy who stopped them in the end. She stood on the far side of the car park, grabbing each of them in turn as they slid towards her.

'We've got to leave!' she yelled. 'We'll miss the last bus.'

Lloyd looked at his watch and saw that she was right. If they hung around any longer, they wouldn't get home. Dinah was already scraping banana peel off her shoes and Harvey was rubbing his face clean with a handkerchief.

'Time to go?' Ian slid to a halt beside them. Mandy nodded and reached out to grab Ingrid.

'We've got to get home, Ing. Do you know where Ellie is?'

Ingrid came to a halt with a graceful half-turn. Then she turned to glance over her shoulder.

And she gasped out loud. 'What's *that*?'

Lloyd looked past her. The great silver shutter had changed. Now there were huge letters shining all over it, shimmering as they spelt out their message.

unmask dj pardoman
see his real face

Ellie slid up to them in reverse, staring back at the letters. 'Have you seen that?' she said.

Everyone else was staring too. The letters began to shimmer faster, morphing into a new message.

tomorrow 5p.m.

'That looks like a website,' Ingrid said 'Why is it up there?'

Lloyd shrugged. 'You'd have to go to the website to find out. But we can't do it until tomorrow.'

'Let's do that,' Ellie said. 'Let's all do it together!' She caught hold of Lloyd's arm and looked round at the others, with fierce, eager eyes. 'Where do you live? I'll come round after school tomorrow.'

3

So—who am I?

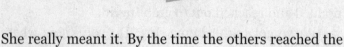

She really meant it. By the time the others reached the Hunters' house after school on Thursday, Ellie was there, waiting. She was leaning against the front door, watching impatiently for them.

'You took your time,' she said sharply.

Lloyd shrugged. 'What's the hurry?'

Quickly, Dinah took out her key. 'Come on in,' she said soothingly. 'I'll go and turn the computer on. How about a cup of tea while we're waiting?'

The others all went into the kitchen, but Ellie tagged along behind Dinah.

'We have to be ready,' she said. 'It's important.'

Dinah didn't like being nagged, but she wasn't going to let herself get rattled. Sitting down in front of the computer, she keyed in the address that had appeared on the shutter.

The site came up straight away, as a purple page full of whirling question marks, glittering silver and lime green.

'It doesn't usually look like *that*!' For a second Ellie sounded startled. Then she raised her voice to call the others. 'Come and see!'

They came crowding into the room, peering over

Dinah's shoulder. Ingrid was hopping excitedly from foot to foot and even Ian was looking enthusiastic.

Dinah began to click on the question marks, following them round to catch them. Each one exploded into a question.

So—who am I?

Where do I come from?

What name did my parents give me?

By the time Dinah had caught every one, the screen was full of unanswered questions. The very last question mark unrolled into an e-mail address and words floated in from the sides to line up underneath it.

Mail me your answers—whoever finds out most about me will be the one to lift off my mask . . . in two weeks' time!

'Wouldn't that be great!' Mandy said. Her eyes were shining. 'No one knows anything about him—not even what he looks like. I'd love to be the one to take off the mask!'

But was DJP really going to let that happen? It didn't make any kind of sense to Dinah. If he was famous for being a mystery, why did he want to ruin all that by being unmasked?

'We've got to go in for the competition,' Ellie said. 'We've got to win.'

Her voice sounded odd to Dinah. Insistent but not emotional. The others obviously didn't hear anything strange though. Lloyd and Ian were studying the questions and Ingrid was squealing in Dinah's ear.

'You can find out about him—can't you, Di? You're

brilliant at things like that! I bet you can beat everyone else—and then we can go to the unmasking!'

Ellie gave Dinah a long, cool look.

'You are going to do it, aren't you?' she said.

Dinah hesitated. 'I don't really—'

'Oh PLEASE!' Ingrid tugged at her sleeve. 'Let's all do it together!'

Dinah sighed. She didn't really want to waste her time on a silly competition, but the others were obviously expecting her to do it. And Ellie's stare was almost like a threat. 'You'll all have to help,' she said slowly. 'It's bound to take ages.'

'Of course we'll help!' Ingrid said. 'Of course, of course, of—'

Ian pushed her off the couch and growled at her. 'Be quiet or I'll eat you up!' Then he looked at the others. 'She's right, though. We ought to go for it. It's a challenge.'

Harvey gave a sudden, excited grin. 'Do you really think we can do it?'

We'll need a lot of luck, Dinah was going to say. But before she got the words out, Mrs Hunter put her head round the door.

'Tea's nearly ready. Would you all like to stay?'

'Yes, *please*!' said Mandy. 'Do we get the banoffi pie?'

'Afraid not.' Mrs Hunter frowned. 'I couldn't get any more bananas—all the shops had sold out. You'll have to make do with rice pudding.'

'My favourite!' said Ian. 'Can I lay the table or something?'

'Well, it's Dinah's turn,' Mrs Hunter said.

Dinah started to get up, but Ingrid beat her to it.

'We'll do it, won't we, Ian?' she said. 'And Harvey can help. That'll give Dinah a bit more time on the computer.'

The four of them dashed out, leaving Mrs Hunter looking startled. 'What's got into Harvey? It was his turn yesterday.'

'He's just got a nice nature,' Lloyd said. He spun Dinah's chair round so that she was facing the keyboard again.

Mrs Hunter shrugged and went out, and Dinah looked down at the keys.

'I suppose we'll have to start on the internet,' she said, talking half to herself. 'But there's going to be an awful lot of stuff.'

'How about trying local things?' Ellie said quickly.

Dinah glanced up to ask what she meant, and Ellie stared back, focused and determined.

'Don't waste time on all the national things,' she said. 'Everyone else is going to find those anyway. Try the local papers for all the places he's visited. I can tell you where he's been.'

Dinah thought for a second. It wasn't a bad idea. No one else was likely to bother with the local sites and they might pick up something unusual. She nodded and pushed a piece of paper towards Ellie. 'OK then. Write me a list of places.' Ellie scribbled for a moment and Dinah watched, taking in the names. Then she leaned forward with one hand on the mouse, concentrating hard.

Lloyd and Mandy tried to watch what she was doing, but she was going very fast and not stopping to explain.

'Why don't we let her get on?' Ellie said.

Lloyd nodded. 'Might as well.'

Dinah hardly heard him. She was busy working out how to set up the right kind of search.

'We'll go and help the others,' Mandy murmured.

Lloyd put a hand on Dinah's shoulder. 'I'll call you when tea's ready.'

Dinah nodded vaguely and clicked on the Search button.

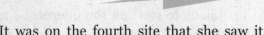

It was on the fourth site that she saw it. Something completely unexpected. It was nothing to do with DJ Pardoman, but it hit her like a punch in the stomach. She sat back and stared at the screen.

THAT can't be there. It can't be. It's impossible.

She was so startled that she didn't realize Lloyd was calling her for tea. She didn't hear a thing until he appeared suddenly in the doorway.

'Di! Are you deaf? I've been shouting for a whole minute.'

Quick as a flash, Dinah minimized the window in front of her. Her heart was thumping as she spun round.

'I'm sorry,' she said. 'I didn't hear you.'

'What were you looking at?' Lloyd said curiously. 'Anything good?'

Dinah shook her head, not quite meeting his eyes. 'Not yet,' she muttered. 'I haven't found anything yet.'

She was so shaken that she could hardly eat. Watching the others chatter and laugh as they ate was like watching something on television. She couldn't keep track of what they were all saying, and she had to struggle to swallow her food.

It can't be true! she kept thinking. *That photograph . . . No! It's impossible. I must have imagined it.*

She shook herself and tried to listen to what Ingrid was saying about DJ Pardoman and the Purple club.

'He's fantastic, Mrs Hunter! He's so-o-o-o fantastic! And Dinah's going to find out all about his life, so that we can unmask him—'

Mr and Mrs Hunter just looked bewildered, but that didn't stop Ingrid talking about DJ Pardoman all through the meal.

Dinah was hoping to sneak back to the computer on her own, but Ellie didn't leave her any chance of that. As soon as the meal was over, she hustled all the others back to the computer, to see what Dinah had found so far.

Oh well, maybe I'll get some time later. Dinah stayed away from the site she was longing to visit and pulled up a selection of others. There was no shortage. She'd already found hundreds and hundreds of reports about DJ Pardoman making personal appearances.

In Norwich . . . in Inverness . . . in Truro . . . in Basingstoke . . .

There were plenty of pictures too. Each one showed the same, strutting figure dressed in sparkling silver—but each one had a different face. Harvey leaned over Dinah's shoulder and read one of the captions.

'*Local teenager Sally Richards chats to DJ Pardoman—the mysterious celebrity who is never seen without his electronic mask.*'

Mandy's eyes gleamed. 'It's a fantastic mystery, isn't it? No one knows what his real face is like.'

'No one knows *anything* about him.' Dinah had seen too many of those pictures already. 'Look.'

She pulled up a few more sites, to let everyone compare them.

. . . the enigmatic DJ with the electronic mask . . .

. . . the star with no face and no biography . . .

. . . the mysterious DJ who hides in a blaze of publicity . . .

. . . is he one of the beautiful people? How can we tell . . . ?

'They're all the same,' she said. 'We're not going to find out anything like this.'

'We might,' Ellie said insistently. 'Keep going.' She knelt down next to Dinah's chair and peered at the screen.

All the others edged closer too. Dinah felt like screaming. *Why don't you go away? I need to do something else! Leave me alone! You're so annoying!*

But that wasn't fair. Ellie was irritating, but the rest

of them weren't. They were SPLAT. Her friends. She ignored the way she felt and made herself grin as she reached for the mouse again.

'OK, I'll go on. But it's pretty boring, I warn you . . . '

She was hoping for some private time with the computer after they'd gone. But she was out of luck again. By the time everyone finally left, Mrs Hunter was muttering dark warnings about going to bed. Reluctantly, Dinah dragged herself upstairs, thinking, *Maybe there'll be a chance tomorrow* . . .

If she'd fallen asleep, she might have managed to wait until then. But at two o'clock, she was still lying awake, with her eyes wide open and her brain buzzing. And the whole house was dark and quiet—except for Harvey, snoring next door.

Slipping out of bed, Dinah inched across her bedroom without turning on the light. She eased open the top drawer of her desk and felt for the little box she kept at the back. When she pulled it out, she didn't need the light. Her fingers knew just how to take off the lid and find the photo inside.

Holding the photo carefully, she crept out of her room and downstairs to the sitting-room. Shutting the door, she listened for a second. When she was sure that Harvey was still snoring, she switched on the standard lamp and started the computer.

Then she laid her photograph down beside the keyboard.

It was a simple holiday snap of a young couple standing together in the sunshine. The man had dark brown eyes, crinkled slightly at the corners. Friendly, smiling eyes. His mouth was smiling too, and his arm was round the waist of the woman beside him.

The other man won't really look anything like that, Dinah thought briskly. *I just imagined it. The moment I put them together, I'll see how different they are.*

She sat down at the computer and typed in an address. Then she waited for the site to come up, feeling tense and a bit sick. It seemed to take for ever to load.

But when it did—it was just as she remembered.

She was looking at the home page of a newspaper's archive site, and it trailed half a dozen stories with brief captions and a picture for each. One was the usual report of a visit by DJ Pardoman—the reason she'd found the site in the first place. It was a perfectly standard report, just like all the others:

. . . the faceless DJ lived up to his man-of-mystery reputation when he paid a call on Sharpley's new store in Maidborough . . . This time, the glittering figure walking through the shop doorway had a face like a Teletubby's, looking slightly blurred.

But there was nothing blurred about the photograph below it—the one that just happened to be on the same page. The face in that was sharp and clear and smiling, with faint crinkles at the corners of the eyes. Dinah picked up her own photo and held it up to the screen, to see the two faces side by side.

And a voice behind her said, 'What are you doing?'

4

THE FACE IN THE PHOTO

'I didn't mean to make you jump,' Lloyd said softly. 'I just wanted to know what was going on.'

'I thought you were all asleep,' Dinah muttered.

Lloyd could see her shaking. What was going on? He walked over to the computer and reached for the mouse. She had minimized the page when she heard his voice, but she hadn't closed it. He brought it up.

For a moment he couldn't understand what was making her look so peculiar. It was just another report about DJ Pardoman, wasn't it?

Then he saw the picture lower down the page—and he understood. This hadn't got anything to do with DJ Pardoman. It was the other picture that had made Dinah tremble. He looked down at the photograph she had put on the desk. Then he looked back at the screen.

'It's your father, isn't it?' he said. 'Your own dad.'

Dinah closed her eyes and took a deep breath. 'But it can't be, can it? He and Mum were both killed in that car accident. When I was a baby.'

Lloyd moved the mouse again, scrolling down to read the caption. The man in the photograph was holding a book. *Local author Phil Ashby proudly displays his new history of Great Ley.*

'You see?' Dinah said lightly. 'It's not my dad. His name was Stephen Glass. This is someone completely different.' She sounded brittle and breathless.

'It's not the same name,' Lloyd said slowly. 'But it's exactly the same face. Hold your photo up next to it.'

The similarity was stunning. Phil Ashby looked a little greyer, and his wrinkles were a bit deeper, but apart from that—it could have been the same picture.

'If that man's not your dad, he's got to be some kind of relation,' Lloyd said at last. 'You ought to get in touch with him.'

'I can't!' Dinah said quickly.

'Why not?'

'He's a stranger. We don't know anything about him. And anyway . . . ' Dinah let her voice trail away.

Lloyd was bewildered. 'What's wrong with you? You haven't got *any* blood relations and suddenly this man turns up looking just like your dad. Don't you *want* to know who he is?'

'Of course I do.' Dinah looked down at her hands. 'But . . . *you're* my family, aren't you? You and Harvey and Mum and Dad. What happens to all that if—if—'

Lloyd knew what she meant. *What happens if Phil Ashby does turn out to be my father . . . ?*

'But you can't just let this go,' he said. 'You've got to find out.'

Dinah sighed miserably. 'What about Mum and Dad?'

'You could tell them.' Lloyd was pretty sure of that. 'It would be all right.'

'But it's a big thing, isn't it?' Dinah said awkwardly.

'And . . . it might be a false alarm. I wish I could check it out before I make a fuss.'

'Well, why don't you?' It didn't sound too difficult to Lloyd. 'We could go to Great Ley and ask a few questions. If he's written a book about the place, there'll be people there who know about him.'

Dinah looked doubtful. 'But it might be right at the other end of the country.'

'Let's do a search.' Lloyd nudged her out of the way and typed in the name. When the results came up, he clicked on the first one with a map and zoomed in. 'Look, there it is. Great Ley. Is it the right one?'

Dinah leaned closer to the screen. 'Yes, it must be. I was looking at the Maidborough Gazette site and Maidborough's only a couple of miles away.'

Lloyd frowned at the map. 'It looks very small.'

'Is it far from here?' Dinah said.

Lloyd shook his head. 'We could probably get there in a couple of hours. If we can get a bus to Maidborough and another one out to Great Ley.' He was itching to make a plan. 'Shall I see if I can find out the bus times?'

He started tapping at the keyboard again and Dinah leaned across to watch. She didn't say anything, but Lloyd could hear how tense she was. She was breathing very fast.

It didn't take long to look up the buses.

'It's easy!' Lloyd was so excited that he forgot to whisper.

'Ssh!' Dinah looked up nervously, but there was no sound except Harvey's snoring.

Lloyd lowered his voice. 'We could go on Saturday. If we leave here at nine, we'll be there by half past ten. And there's a good bus back around five.'

'But what about the others?' Dinah frowned. 'They'll think it's funny if we go off on a Saturday without them.'

'Without the others?' That hadn't even occurred to Lloyd. He stared at Dinah. 'Won't they be coming too?'

'No!' Dinah said fiercely.

'But—'

'*No!* You're not to tell them!'

Lloyd couldn't believe his ears. 'But . . . we're SPLAT. We stick together.'

'I know. But this is different.' Dinah looked down at her fingers. 'I'll just go on my own.'

'Don't be stupid.' Lloyd knew he couldn't let her do that. 'You can't go *completely* on your own. It wouldn't be safe. Let me come with you, even if no one else does.'

'I suppose—' Dinah hesitated for a second. Then she nodded. 'OK. Thanks. Just the two of us then.'

'If you say so.' Lloyd pulled a face. 'But we'll have to think up a really good cover story.'

He glanced up at the ceiling. Above their heads, Harvey's snores rattled peacefully on.

5

IAN'S PLAN

Dinah spent the rest of the night trying to think of a good excuse to go off without the others on Saturday. But she needn't have worried.

When they met at school the next morning, Ian was grinning all over his face. 'I looked up all those sites you found, Di. Got up specially early this morning to do it. And I've made a list.' He took a piece of paper out of his pocket.

'A list of what?' Dinah said cautiously.

Ian's grin widened. 'You know that picture all the local papers had?'

'You mean *Enigmatic DJ chats to local teenagers*?' Ingrid pulled a face.

Ian nodded triumphantly. 'Well—I've made a list of the teenagers! I think we ought to go and talk to them!'

'Maybe we should,' Dinah said. She tried to let him down gently. 'But how are we going to find them?'

Ian looked smug. 'Think about it. What do we know about teenagers who follow DJP?'

'They're keen on music?' Mandy said.

Ian shook his head impatiently. 'What else?'

'Sociable?' said Ingrid.

Ian nodded. 'Probably. So they're likely to be around

in the town centre on Saturday morning. And how are we going to spot them?'

Dinah drew a long breath. 'They wear really old clothes,' she said. 'And Purple make-up.'

'That's right!' Ian said. 'Thank goodness someone's got brains.' He waved his piece of paper. 'We know these people are all teenagers from towns quite near here. We know what they—and their friends—are likely to wear. So we can go and ask around for them.'

'You really think that will work?' Harvey said doubtfully.

Ian sighed. 'Of course it will. If these actual people aren't around, some of their friends are bound to be. If we split up and go to different towns, we're sure to find *someone*.'

'Suppose we do,' said Ingrid. 'What do we do then?'

'We ask them about DJP, of course!' Ian said impatiently. 'How he got there. If they've got his autograph. What he had for lunch—stuff like that. If we keep asking, there's bound to be something that gives us a lead.'

It all sounded pretty far-fetched to Dinah. Even if they did find those teenagers—what could they possibly have to say? She tried to think of a kind way to tell Ian it wouldn't work.

But before she could speak, Lloyd took her by surprise. He suddenly beamed enthusiastically.

'Brilliant!' he said. 'We'll do it tomorrow. If we split into pairs, we can go to three different places.'

Dinah blinked. He thought it was a good idea?

'What about Ellie?' Mandy said. 'We promised she could join in.'

'She'll have to go with you,' Lloyd said. He looked round at the others. 'You can take Harvey too. Then Ian and Ingrid can go together—and Dinah and I will be the other pair.'

Mandy nodded slowly, but Ingrid didn't look convinced.

'It'll have to be somewhere close,' she said grumpily. 'Or I won't be able to pay the fare.'

'The fares could probably come out of SPLAT funds.' Lloyd glanced at Ian. 'Can we afford it?'

Ian looked even more triumphant. 'I checked that out before breakfast too. As long as we don't go further than fifty miles, there's enough to pay for everyone's tickets. And there's loads of places . . .'

He was still explaining when the bell rang. They set off into school but Dinah loitered behind. She wanted to know what Lloyd was up to.

He was looking very pleased with himself. 'Wasn't that a fantastic bit of luck?' he said, as soon as the others were out of earshot. 'Now we can go to Great Ley tomorrow.'

'But that's not right,' Dinah said. 'We can't use SPLAT funds for that. It would be cheating!'

'No it wouldn't.' Lloyd looked offended. 'We'll ask around for Ian's people first, of course. But then we can go on to Great Ley.'

Dinah still wasn't happy about it.

'Look,' Lloyd said crossly. 'You want to go to Great

Ley. And you're desperate not to tell the others. Right? Well—I've fixed it so you can do that. You ought to be grateful. If you're worried about wasting SPLAT funds, you'd better work out some good questions to ask these teenagers of Ian's. *If* we find any of them.' He stomped off.

Dinah sighed. Lloyd was right, of course. It was a wonderful chance to do what she wanted. She just hoped the others didn't have a pointless day. She went into school, thinking up questions as hard as she could.

That mask. What's it made of? When does he take it on and off?

How do people book a personal appearance by him?

Does he arrive alone—or has he got a manager who comes too?

There were plenty of things to ask. But she wasn't sure they were going to get any answers.

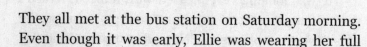

They all met at the bus station on Saturday morning. Even though it was early, Ellie was wearing her full Purple make-up.

'When did *you* get up?' Ingrid said. 'That must take ages to do. I'd rather stay in bed a bit longer.'

Ellie looked her up and down, scornfully. 'It's important,' she said. 'It shows I'm a First Purple. I was there on the opening night—when DJP was there *himself*, with his roadies and his manager and everyone. First Purples are *special*.'

Ingrid tossed her head. 'We're all going to be special. When we win this competition and unmask DJP. We—'

'Sssh!' Ellie hissed. She looked round quickly. 'Don't forget—everyone else wants to win too. We mustn't let them steal our ideas!'

There was something frightening about her cold intensity. Dinah couldn't wait to leave her behind, and she was relieved when the Maidborough bus drew up beside them.

'Let's go, Lloyd,' she said.

They both jumped on to the bus and Lloyd let his breath out noisily as it pulled away. 'Thank goodness *we* haven't got to put up with Ellie all day. She's a real weirdo, isn't she?'

'I just don't understand why she behaves like that,' Dinah said. 'As if the competition really *matters*.'

Lloyd shrugged. 'Who cares? We've got enough to do without worrying about her. We'll have to work fast when we get to Maidborough. Otherwise we won't make it to Great Ley.'

'We mustn't skimp on the searching,' Dinah said. 'We've let SPLAT pay our fares. We can't go to Great Ley until we've found—what are their names?'

Lloyd had them written down. 'Melanie Chirt and Dennis Ryan.'

'Melanie and Dennis.' Dinah looked down at the names, memorizing them. 'Let's hope we find them quickly. Maidborough's not a very big place. Most of the kids must know each other from school.'

That sounded quite logical on the bus.

But it didn't seem to help much when they were actually in Maidborough. Lloyd felt horribly embarrassed as he wandered round the shops, forcing himself to speak to every teenager in ragged clothes and heavy make-up.

'Hi. You don't happen to know Dennis Ryan, do you? . . . Hi—I'm looking for Dennis Ryan . . . Hi . . .'

Out of the corner of his eye he could see Dinah, over on the other side of the shop. She was trying the same thing with the girls.

'Excuse me. Do you know Melanie Chirt? . . . Hello. Is Melanie Chirt anywhere around?'

Dinah was the first to have any luck—if you could call it luck. After half an hour or so, she stopped a girl who gave a sniff and tossed her head.

'I *ought* to know Melanie. She is my best friend, after all. Who wants her?'

'It's about DJ Pardoman,' Dinah said. 'We wanted to ask Melanie—'

'Oh, you can't *talk* to her!' The girl looked gleeful. She was obviously the sort of person who liked giving bad news. 'Melanie's just gone off to New Zealand for three weeks, to stay with her dad.'

We can cross her off, then, Dinah thought gloomily. She went to join Lloyd as he ploughed on, asking for Dennis Ryan. No one would tell them anything about him. They just sniggered.

'Looking for Dennis? You must be crazy.'

'What do you want him for?'

By lunchtime, Lloyd and Dinah were both feeling

downhearted. They took a break and phoned the others, to see how they were getting on.

Talking to Ian and Ingrid certainly didn't cheer them up.

'It's all a waste of time!' Ingrid said fiercely. 'We've only found one of our people and she doesn't know a *thing*. And we've been to the shopping mall, but we can't get into the supermarket DJP opened. It's all boarded up. The windows got smashed on Wednesday, because there weren't any bananas.'

'We're not giving up yet,' Ian said gruffly. 'We're going back to the mall this afternoon.'

Lloyd heard a scornful sniff and he guessed that Ingrid had been arguing about that.

Mandy and Harvey and Ellie hadn't got anything to report either.

'We found a girl who'd *heard* of our boy,' Mandy said. 'But she didn't know where to find him.'

'We'll try again this afternoon,' Ellie said, breaking in. 'There'll be different people in the shops then.'

Harvey grunted miserably in the background and Lloyd pulled a face as he switched off his phone.

'You see?' Dinah was starting to feel guilty again. 'We've just been wasting time and money, haven't we?'

'It's not over yet,' said Lloyd. 'Remember—we only need one clue to start us off. The others might discover something this afternoon. There's loads of time left.'

He tapped his watch to prove it—and gave a yelp.

'It's almost half past one! If we don't hurry, we'll miss the bus to Great Ley. Come on. I'll race you.'

He set off at top speed and Dinah was left standing. She thought she heard a voice shout behind her, but she had no time to look round. Lloyd had just swung round the corner and she didn't want to lose him. She started after him, running as fast as she could.

They were both out of breath when they reached the bus station. It took them a couple of minutes to find the right bus for Great Ley. By the time they had tracked it down, its engine was already running.

'Quick!' Lloyd said.

He pushed Dinah ahead of him, through the open doors of the bus. As she scrambled into a seat, she heard the sound of running feet. She looked through the window—and saw a heavy hand land on Lloyd's shoulder.

'Here!' said a belligerent voice. 'I want a word with you!'

It was a huge boy with an ugly scowl on his face. He was a head taller than Lloyd and twice as broad, with massive shoulders and arms like mechanical grabs. Lloyd spun round and Dinah saw his eyes open very wide.

'You're making a mistake—' he began.

The boy shook his head firmly. 'No mistake. You've been going round asking for me. Right?'

'I—' Lloyd started to shake his head. But then, suddenly, his face lit up. 'You're Dennis Ryan!'

Of course! Dinah thought. As the boy nodded, she started to slide out of her seat. But she was too late. The bus doors closed with a snap and the bus began to pull away from the stop.

She was off to Great Ley on her own after all.

6

DENNIS RYAN

He'd missed the bus! Lloyd stared after it as it disappeared round the corner. He couldn't believe it.

'What's up?' said Dennis Ryan. 'Lost your girlfriend?'

'She's not my girlfriend,' Lloyd said. 'She's my sister.'

He turned back to Dennis—and felt the shock of his size all over again. It was terrifying. Dennis was the largest boy he'd ever seen—and he was looking distinctly aggressive. Lloyd took a step back.

That was a mistake. Dennis reached out and grabbed him by the jacket, lifting him off his feet.

'OK,' he growled. 'What I want to know is—what are you after?'

'I'm n-n-not—'

'Don't try and get out of it.' Dennis gave him a shake. 'All my mates kept saying, *There's a boy looking for you*. But when I caught up with you and called out—you ran away! So what's up? You want a fight?'

He gave the front of the jacket another shake.

'Of c-c-c-course I d-d-don't.' Lloyd had to struggle to get the words out. 'We just want-t-t-ted to t-t-t-talk.'

'Talk? You want to talk to *me*?' Dennis was so startled that he let go of the jacket.

Lloyd crashed back to the ground and he had to

stagger to keep his footing. 'We saw your name in the paper,' he said, when he'd got his breath back.

Dennis looked mystified. 'Me? In the paper?'

'When you met DJ Pardoman.'

'Oh, HEY!' Dennis stopped glowering and his face lit up. 'That DJP! What a man! Isn't he great?'

'Is he like that in real life?' Lloyd said. 'Does he wear that mask thing all the time?'

Dennis nodded. 'Every second. He was wearing it when he arrived.'

'How did he come?' Lloyd was struggling to remember Dinah's questions. 'Did he drive himself? Or did he have a chauffeur?'

Dennis shook his head. 'He didn't come by car.'

'No car?' Lloyd hadn't expected that.

'He came in a *boat*!' Dennis said gleefully. 'We were all looking the other way, waiting for a limo, and suddenly—WHOOSH!' His eyes gleamed. He was re-living his moment of glory. 'We were all in Sharpley's car park, watching the road. The other kids had shoved me right to the back, by the canal—'

'There's a canal there?' Lloyd tried to picture it.

'I'll show you!' Dennis said, grabbing Lloyd's arm. He started to haul him out of the bus station. 'It won't take a minute.'

There was no point in resisting. Lloyd couldn't have dragged his arm free if he'd wanted to. And anyway, why not look at the canal? He had nothing else to do until Dinah's bus came back from Great Ley.

Dennis pulled him along the pavement and down the hill, talking all the time.

'Everyone says I go on about DJP too much. But they're just jealous. They reckoned they had it all sewn up. *They* were the ones lined up at the kerb. *They* were the ones who were going to talk to him. *They* were the ones looking up the road for the limo. But who got to meet him in the end? Dumb old Dennis! Because suddenly there was this WHOOSH!—'

Lloyd really wanted to hear the story in the car park where it happened. But he didn't dare interrupt Dennis again, so he listened as hard as he could, and tried to remember the details.

He needn't have worried. Dennis loved telling the story so much that when he got to the end he went straight back and began again. And again.

By the time they reached Sharpley's, he was telling it all for the third time. '—and the boat stopped with, like, a tidal wave. And he came jumping up with his hands held out to me. *Hey, man! How're you doin'?*'

For the third time, Dennis put his head on one side and held out his hands, playing at being DJ Pardoman. It was a perfect, practised performance. He must have done it hundreds of times before.

This performance finished right outside the store— and, finally, Lloyd understood what had happened. Sharpley's was on the main shopping street, with a big car park behind it. Anyone arriving by car would have swept straight into the car park. For someone as important as DJP, there would have been a parking space reserved, right by the building, and that was where the crowd would have gathered.

Lloyd could see it all now. Hundreds of kids pushing forward, desperate to meet DJP and hear his voice. All trying to glimpse the face behind the mask. Dennis had been shuffled back to the far side of the car park—because he might be scarily big, but he wasn't all that tough once you got to know him.

So he'd landed up right next to the canal.

He was already dragging Lloyd across to see the place. It wasn't very impressive. Just a stretch of old, dirty canal, separated from the car park by a low, dilapidated fence.

'Right up there—' Dennis pointed up the canal. '—there was a WHOOSH! And then he was here. Before anyone could move. You don't get boats on the canal much, and they're usually really slow. But this one—it stopped with, like, a tidal wave. And he came jumping up—'

Lloyd heard it through once more, to the very end. Then he started asking questions. 'What happened to the boat? Did he tie it up?'

Dennis shook his head. 'It went up to the canal basin, turned round and—WHOOSH! It went back the way it came.'

'He wasn't driving it himself then?' Lloyd seized on that. 'So who was?'

'Some man,' Dennis said vaguely. 'He just drove the boat off, and DJP—'

But Lloyd didn't want to hear the same old story

again. He concentrated on the boat. There might be a clue there. 'What about when DJP left? Did the boat come back? Was the same man driving it?'

Solemnly, Dennis shook his head. 'He didn't go away like that. He just—vanished.'

'*Vanished?*' Lloyd forgot all about the boat. He stared at Dennis. 'What do you mean?'

'He disappeared. Pfff!' Dennis waved his hands in the air. 'He went into the shop—to do the opening—and we all stood round the building waiting to see him when he left. We were *all the way* round.'

'And you didn't see him come out?'

Solemnly, Dennis shook his head. 'He didn't come. They shut the place up and told us he'd gone, but we didn't believe them. So we went on waiting. He never came.'

Lloyd shrugged. 'He must have taken off his mask and changed his clothes. Then he just walked out and you didn't recognize him.'

Dennis looked triumphant. 'That's not what the store supervisor said!'

'What was that?' Lloyd said patiently.

'*I showed him into my office and stopped outside to get him some coffee. When I went in—*' Dennis paused dramatically. '*—he wasn't there! He couldn't have got past me without being seen*. That's what the supervisor said. I heard it on the TV. *He couldn't have got past—not unless he hypnotized me.*'

'But that's ridiculous,' Lloyd said. 'He can't have—'

And then the words sank in. He took a long, slow breath. '*What* did the supervisor say?'

'I reckon it was a joke.' Dennis looked knowing. 'The supervisor hadn't got a clue what happened. Made a joke, so as not to look an idiot. *He couldn't have got past—not unless he hypnotized me.* That makes it a mystery, see.'

He began to make rhythmic movements in the air, opening and closing his hands and pushing them backwards and forwards at Lloyd's face.

'You. Are. In. My. Power,' he chanted in a melodramatic voice. 'You. Will. Not. See. Me. When. I. Come. Past. Hypnotize! HYPNOTIZE!!!' He was grinning from ear to ear and rolling his eyes as he spoke.

But it wasn't like that. *You've got it wrong,* Lloyd wanted to say. *Hypnotism's not funny.*

There was another face looming in his mind. A stern, cruel face with pale lips and paper-white skin. He could see another pair of eyes, not rolling like Dennis's but fixed and ice-cold. Strange, luminous, sea-green eyes that tried to see right inside your mind.

The Headmaster's eyes.

Lloyd could hear the Headmaster's voice in his mind as well. It wasn't comic and robotic, like Dennis's. It was soft and emotionless—and very frightening. *Funny that you should be feeling so sleepy . . .*

But DJP couldn't be the Headmaster! He *couldn't*! For a moment, Lloyd forgot where he was and what he was doing.

When he came to himself again, he found Dennis bending down to peer anxiously into his face.

'I didn't do it, did I?' he said. 'I didn't really hypnotize you?'

'Of course not,' Lloyd said, with an effort. 'No one can hypnotize me. Not even—' But it was better not to talk about the Headmaster. He forced a friendly smile on to his face. 'Thank you for telling me about DJP.'

'I can tell you again,' Dennis said eagerly. 'I don't mind.'

'No, that's fine. Honestly.' Lloyd backed away. He had to get off by himself to work things out. 'You've been really great and it was very interesting. Thanks.'

He gave a last grin and a wave, and dived into Sharpley's, ducking in between shelves so that Dennis wouldn't follow him.

His brain was spinning. Had DJ Pardoman really hypnotized the supervisor? Or was Dennis right when he said it was just a joke?

He had to find out. And he couldn't wait for Dinah to come back from Great Ley. It would be too late by then. If he was going to ask questions, he'd have to do it on his own. And he would need an excuse . . .

He stuck his head out of the store, looked left and right—to make sure that Dennis wasn't around—and then walked briskly up the road to hunt for a stationery shop.

When he found one, he bought a pen and paper and a clipboard. He made a few scribbled notes, so that the paper on the clipboard wasn't completely blank. Then he went back to Sharpley's and joined the queue at the counter.

'Please can I see the supervisor?' he said, when he reached the front. 'There's a project I'm doing—' It wasn't a very good excuse, but he couldn't think of anything better.

The supervisor was a tall skinny blonde with spiky hair. She was wearing jeans and heavy boots and she looked him up and down coldly.

'You can have ten minutes. OK? But you won't get any freebies—whatever the project is.'

'I'm not after freebies,' Lloyd said quickly. 'I just want to ask a few questions.'

'Well crack on then. I'm serious about the ten minutes.'

Lloyd gabbled through a couple of dull, ordinary questions. (*How long have you done this job? What did you do before?*) Then he tried to get her on to the right subject.

'What's the most exciting thing that's happened since you came?'

She didn't hesitate. 'The day the shop nearly burned down.'

Drat! Lloyd thought. He tried again.

'What drew the biggest crowds?'

The supervisor considered for a moment. 'When we had that rumour Madonna was coming.'

Double drat! Lloyd felt his ten minutes ticking away. He couldn't waste any more time being subtle. He would have to ask straight out.

'And didn't you have a visit from DJ Pardoman?'

'That's right.' She looked hard at Lloyd. 'He was here about six months ago.'

Lloyd knew the date perfectly well, but he made a quick note, to avoid suspicion. 'And was there anything—special about the visit?'

'He turned up in a speedboat—after I'd spent ages arranging for the police to hold up the traffic for him.'

'What about—when he left?' Lloyd was trying to sound super-casual now. 'Anything special about that?'

The supervisor looked him straight in the eye. 'I am not able to give out any more information about DJ Pardoman,' she said.

There was something about the way she said it that made Lloyd uneasy. Quickly he tried another question.

'Could you just tell me—did he take off his mask when he had a drink?'

The supervisor's eyes didn't waver. 'I am not able to give out any more information about DJ Pardoman,' she said again.

Lloyd felt a shiver run down his spine. 'Well—can't you tell me how you made the booking for him to come?'

The answer didn't change. 'I am not able to give out any more information about DJ Pardoman.'

'But all I want to know is—'

Too late. The supervisor looked down at her watch.

'Time's up!' she said crisply. 'Hope you got what you wanted, because that's all you're getting. And tell your school not to send any more people. I can't stand around answering questions all day.'

She stomped off and Lloyd stood staring after her. It was a moment or two before he realized that he hadn't written down the thing he most needed to remember.

He left a space and printed the words so that they stood out clearly.

I am not able to give out any more information about DJ Pardoman.

7

GREAT LEY

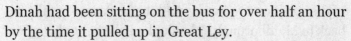

Dinah had been sitting on the bus for over half an hour by the time it pulled up in Great Ley.

She was expecting a pretty little village, with a shop and a post office. Maybe there would even be a church and a village green. She was sure she could stroll round and get talking to people.

But Great Ley wasn't like that at all. It was a small modern estate, dumped down by the side of the main road. Dinah's heart sank as she climbed off the bus. She couldn't see anything except brick boxes with huge garages and tiny gardens. It wasn't the sort of place where people stood around chatting.

She was still wondering when the bus pulled away. That settled one thing anyway. She couldn't get back to Maidborough for hours, so she might as well explore. There was nothing else to do.

She set off to walk round the estate. It didn't take long. The main street was a loop and there were half a dozen cul-de-sacs opening off it—maybe a hundred houses in all. And that was it. No shops, no pub, no sign of life. She walked as slowly as she could, keeping her eyes open, but she didn't see a single person. The whole place was deserted.

Dinah felt like sitting down on the pavement and bursting into tears. It wasn't fair! How could Phil Ashby have written a book about such a dull, useless place? She had been really sure she would find out something about him by coming to Great Ley, but it was obviously hopeless.

And what was she going to do now? Sit at the side of the road for two hours until the bus came to take her back to Maidborough? That looked like her only option.

But she couldn't even do that. While she was looking for a place to sit, the temperature dropped suddenly and it started to rain. There was no kind of shelter at the bus stop, not even a tree. If she sat still, she would get soaked and cold.

There *had* to be something else to do! In desperation, she went back to the bus stop to check the timetable. Maybe—just maybe—there was an earlier bus back to Maidborough. One that she and Lloyd somehow hadn't noticed.

There wasn't. But she saw two words on the timetable that caught her eye. *High Ley.* The buses that stopped at Great Ley made another stop there, five minutes later. Maybe there was a shop at High Ley where she could shelter. There might even be someone who could answer her questions.

At the very least, if she headed that way, she would be walking and not standing still in the rain.

She took one last look at the raw new bricks of Great Ley and then she pulled up her hood and started to walk.

It took her half an hour—uphill—and by the time she reached High Ley she was tired as well as cold and wet.

To begin with, the place didn't look any more promising than Great Ley. But after she had squelched past half a dozen bungalows she found herself in a proper village centre with five or six old houses and a dingy shop with a handwritten notice in the window.

**SORRY NO FLOUR
OR BANANAS
OR GOLDEN SYRUP**

There was a little library too. And it was open. *Tuesdays and Saturdays—2.00 p.m. to 7.00 p.m.* Dinah almost cheered. It was exactly what she wanted. She pushed the door open and went in.

Inside, there were a couple of women sitting on the floor by the picture book box, reading to their toddlers. Three old women were scanning the shelves and chatting to each other. And there were six teenage boys huddled round the computer.

'You're wet!' said the library assistant brightly, as Dinah came in.

Dinah took out her tissue and dried her face. 'I've just walked up from Great Ley.'

'Walked? In this weather?' The library assistant looked astounded. 'Why didn't you get the bus?'

It was too complicated to explain. Dinah just

shrugged. 'I'm looking for the history of Great Ley. By Phil Ashby. Have you got it?'

'Sure to have,' the library assistant said. 'This isn't my job—I'm just filling in for someone who's ill—but there's bound to be a copy in the reference section.'

She came out from behind the counter and began to hunt along the shelves. It didn't take her long to find what she was looking for.

'There you are. I'm afraid you can't borrow it, but it won't take you long to read.'

'Thank you.' Dinah took the little book and hesitated. 'And . . . er . . . do you know anything about the author? Phil Ashby.'

The library assistant shook her head. 'Sorry. This isn't my area. I usually work over on the other side of Maidborough. You could try coming in on Tuesday and talking to Julie. She ought to be better by then.'

'Right. Thank you.'

Dinah was too disappointed to say anything else. She went and sat down at the little table in the middle of the library. The book wasn't very long. If she read it quickly, perhaps she could go to the shop. Surely the people there would be local. They might know something.

She opened the book and scanned the first sentence. *Long ago, in the fourteenth century, the village of Great Ley was wiped out by the Black Death.* But she couldn't concentrate. The words jumbled themselves together and danced on the page in front of her.

She was re-reading the same page for the third time when a hesitant voice beside her said, 'Excuse me . . .'

It was one of the women who'd been looking at picture books. Dinah smiled.

'Hello,' she said.

The woman smiled back and sat down. 'Hello. I'm Jane. I hope you don't mind, but I heard you asking about Phil Ashby.'

Dinah's heart gave a thump. 'Do you know him?'

Jane grinned. 'I ought to. He's my lodger. Why did you want to know about him?'

'Because—' For a second, Dinah was utterly tongue-tied. She didn't know where to start. 'I think he might be . . . a relation of mine,' she said at last.

'You're tracing your family tree?' Jane smiled apologetically. 'Well, you've made a mistake about Phil, I'm afraid. Ashby's not his real name.'

'Isn't it?' Suddenly Dinah could hardly breathe. 'What *is* his real name then?'

'That's just it. He doesn't—'

But before Jane could explain, her little boy fell over the pile of books he had been making. He started to wail at the top of his voice and Jane jumped up and went back to the book box to rescue him. Dinah followed her. She wasn't going to let the conversation stop there.

'It wasn't the *name* that put me on to Phil Ashby,' she said, when she could make herself heard over the wailing. 'It was his face. I saw his picture in the paper and—and he looks incredibly like my father.'

That sounded very feeble to her. But Jane's face lit up suddenly. 'You mean you recognized his face? *Really?*'

Dinah was taken aback. 'Well—sort of.'

'But that's wonderful!' Jane said. 'He'll be so happy.' Then her grin faded. 'At least, he will be if—' Her voice trailed away.

'Why happy?' Dinah said.

'Because he'll be able to find out who he is!' Jane sat down on the floor with her little boy on her lap. She opened a picture book to distract him. 'Look at the duck, Freddy! He's got red boots on!'

Dinah's heart was pounding. She sat down beside Jane. 'You mean—he doesn't *know* who he is?'

Jane nodded. 'He turned up here about a year ago. When we advertised a room to let. (Yes, Fred, it *is* a duck.) He's a really nice man, but he's completely lost his long-term memory.'

Dinah swallowed hard. 'You don't know—when that happened, do you?'

'Not sure.' Jane frowned. 'It must have been quite a while back, because he says he worked on the Great Ley estate when they were building it. It feels like home to him because it's more or less the first place he can remember. That's why he wrote the book about it.'

'So—when was the estate built?' Dinah was almost whispering now.

Jane considered. 'Well, we've been there nine years. (Quack, quack, quack, Freddy.) And the house wasn't quite new when we bought it.'

Dinah closed her eyes. Very carefully, she repeated all the things Jane had said. 'So—he's lost his memory? And it was more than nine years ago?'

Jane nodded. 'More than ten, I think.'

'And Phil Ashby isn't his real name?' Dinah's heart was racing. It was tempting to make a great leap. If the man in the picture wasn't really called Phil Ashby—if he didn't know who he was—if he'd lost his memory more than ten years ago—then maybe, just maybe—

But she didn't let herself finish the thought. She wasn't going to make guesses. She wasn't going to think anything at all until the facts were absolutely clear.

She opened her eyes again. 'Do you think it would be possible—do you think he would mind—if I came round to your house to talk to him?'

Jane looked up sharply from the picture book. 'Talk to him? But don't you know—I thought you'd seen his photograph in the paper?'

'I did,' Dinah said. 'He was holding his book about Great Ley.'

Jane looked horrified. 'Oh dear. I didn't know you meant *that* picture. I'm so sorry.' She put a hand on Dinah's arm. 'I'm afraid this is going to be a bit of a shock.'

'What's the matter?' Dinah said quickly.

'I thought you'd seen the picture they had in last week's paper. So I thought you knew. He—' Jane bit her lip. 'He crashed his car and he's in Maidborough Hospital. In Intensive Care.'

'Is he badly injured?' Dinah said stupidly.

'They don't know if he's going to live to the end of the week.'

8

PHIL ASHBY

Lloyd was standing at the bus stop, waiting for Dinah to get back from Great Ley. As soon as she got off the bus, he grabbed her arm.

'Di—thank goodness you're back! I've found out something terrible—'

Dinah blinked at him. 'You mean—you know already?' she said.

What on earth was she talking about?

'Of course I know,' Lloyd said impatiently. 'And I'm trying to tell you.' He launched into a long explanation of what he'd discovered.

' . . . I didn't believe it when Dennis told me, but when I talked to the store supervisor she was just like that. She kept saying: *I am not able to give out any more information about DJ Pardoman.* Just as if—'

Dinah was looking very confused. Lloyd shook her arm.

'Don't you get it?' he said fiercely.

'Get what?' Dinah said. 'I'm sorry, I can't—'

'Don't be stupid. He hypnotized her. DJP hypnotized the store supervisor!' Lloyd shook her arm again. 'Don't you see what that means? *It's the Headmaster.*'

That woke Dinah up with a shock. '*What's* the

Headmaster? What are you talking about?'

Lloyd took a deep breath and said it as clearly as he could. 'I think DJ Pardoman is the Headmaster.' There was a horrible silence. Then Dinah said, 'But—he can't be.'

Lloyd knew how she felt. Last time they'd seen the Headmaster, he'd been going off in an ambulance. He'd collapsed trying to download all the knowledge in the world into his own brain, so that he could take control of everything. Instead of seizing power, he'd collapsed—and no one thought he would ever recover.

But—DJP had hypnotized that woman in Sharpley's. And now he was planning a grand unmasking, watched by millions of people.

'Don't you see?' Lloyd said grimly. 'That's just the sort of thing the Headmaster would do. All the clubs will be packed out that night. That means hundreds of thousands of people watching.'

Dinah began to take it in. 'No, it's worse than that. Because it's going to be live on the News as well. Everyone who's not in one of the clubs will be watching on television.'

Lloyd nodded slowly. 'It'll be an ideal opportunity to take control of the whole country, won't it? DJP's mask will come off—and everyone will be staring straight into his eyes!'

'And if he *is* the Headmaster—he'll hypnotize them,' said Dinah.

'Just the way he hypnotized the woman in Sharpley's.' Lloyd pulled a face. 'You should have heard her. *I am not able to give out any more information about DJ Pardoman*. That was all I could get out of her. Every time I asked a question.'

Dinah was still thinking about it. 'It sounds like the Headmaster all right. But—could he *really* be DJP? Can you imagine him strutting about on a stage like that? And keeping up to date with the music?'

'He'll do anything to get power!' Lloyd said. 'You know he will! We've got to tell the others as soon as we can, and make a plan to stop him! We'll get the next bus out of here—'

'No.' Dinah looked pale, but she said it quite steadily.

Lloyd stared at her. 'What do you mean?'

'I can't leave Maidborough yet. I have to go to the hospital.' Dinah bit her lip. 'Phil Ashby's had an accident.'

Lloyd suddenly remembered what she had been doing while he was investigating—and he felt terrible. 'I'm sorry. I should have asked you what happened.'

'He's in Intensive Care.' Dinah's voice was starting to shake and she was even paler now.

Lloyd tried to think sensibly. 'Is it really a good idea to visit him while he's so ill? He might think you're pestering him about nothing.'

'It's *not* nothing,' Dinah said. 'He—his name's not really Phil Ashby. He's lost his memory. He doesn't know *who* he really is.'

Lloyd hadn't expected that. 'You think there was a mistake?' he said slowly. 'About your parents' accident?'

'Suppose it wasn't my father's body in the car after all.' Dinah looked half-scared of what she was saying. 'Suppose he and my mum picked up a hitchhiker. *He* could have been the second body. And my dad could have lost his memory and wandered off.'

It sounded horribly plausible. 'You've got to find out, haven't you?' Lloyd said. 'But shouldn't you wait until he comes out of hospital?'

'That's just it,' Dinah said faintly. 'He might not come out. They don't know if he'll live to the end of the week.'

Lloyd hesitated for a second. Then he nodded. 'OK. I'll come with you. Let's go and find out how to get there.'

The hospital was vast and new, a great slab of a building with seven floors and wings going off on both sides. Lloyd stood in the main entrance and studied the big plan on the wall.

'It's not too bad really. The corridors are colour-coded and there are lifts just down there. But we need to go to the main reception desk, to find out where he is.'

They had to go up to the third floor and along a blue corridor. That led them to a pair of double doors.

INTENSIVE CARE.
NO ENTRY WITHOUT PERMISSION
PLEASE RING AND WAIT
UNTIL SOMEONE COMES.
IT IS NOT ALWAYS POSSIBLE
TO ANSWER IMMEDIATELY.
PLEASE WAIT.

Lloyd rang the bell.

After five minutes, a nurse opened the left-hand door and peered round it. She looked them up and down but she didn't let them in.

'Yes?' she said.

'We've come to see Phil Ashby,' said Lloyd.

The nurse smiled apologetically. 'I'm afraid we don't allow visiting by unaccompanied children.'

'But—' Dinah gulped and stopped.

Lloyd could tell that she was on the verge of tears. 'She's his daughter,' he said, abruptly. 'You've got to let her in.'

Dinah caught her breath.

The nurse looked more sympathetic, but she still didn't let them in. 'Can't she come with her mother?'

'Her mother's dead,' Lloyd said. It sounded very bald, but he didn't dare to try and explain.

'And we can't come back again today,' Dinah muttered. 'So if we wait until tomorrow, will he still be—will we be too late?'

The nurse hesitated. Then she stepped back and held the door open. 'Well—come in just for a minute or two. But you'll need to be very calm and sensible. He's hooked up to a lot of tubes and he isn't conscious. There's really not a lot of point—'

She beckoned them down the corridor. There were two small wards, one opening off each side of the corridor. Leading them to the left-hand ward, she peeped in and then opened the door.

'Come on. He's in the bed in the far corner. Make sure you're really quiet.'

Lloyd nodded, and he and Dinah tiptoed past the first two beds and into the corner.

'You won't get much conversation out of him,' the nurse said in a low voice. 'But he's holding on. He might even be a tiny bit better today.'

The figure on the bed was completely motionless. He was partly hidden behind the nurse and it wasn't until Lloyd and Dinah walked past her, to the foot of the bed, that they got the full picture.

The man's head was swathed in bandages which hid his face completely. Dozens of tubes trailed from his body and neck and from under the bandages, linking him to a bank of drips and monitors. It was a daunting sight.

Lloyd took a step backwards. 'Is he going to die?' he said.

The nurse gave him a warning look. 'Be careful what you say,' she murmured. 'People in a coma can sometimes hear you very well.'

'I wish they could speak too,' Dinah said. She stood looking down at the man on the bed, staring at his white, bandaged head.

Lloyd wondered what she could see. It might have been anyone lying there; the head was completely shapeless, padded out grotesquely over the nose and under the chin. He couldn't see the point of gazing at something like that, when the person was unconscious. But Dinah stared on and on, without moving.

Lloyd let her stand there for as long as he dared. But in the end he had to disturb her. 'Di? We've got to go now, or we'll miss our bus home.'

'Mmm?' Dinah glanced at her watch. 'Oh. Sorry.'

They walked up the ward together. As they passed the desk, the nurse who had let them in looked up at Dinah.

'Feel better now you've seen him?'

'I—I think so,' Dinah said uncertainly.

The nurse stared at her for a moment. Then she said, 'You can come again if you want to. You're no bother. If there's someone else on duty, just tell them that Bernadette said it was all right.'

'Thanks,' Dinah muttered.

Lloyd found it hard to get her out of the ward. She stopped in the doorway and glanced back, as though the figure on the bed might suddenly sit up and wave to her.

'Come on,' Lloyd said. 'We've got to go.'

Reluctantly, Dinah followed him through the double doors and down the blue corridor.

She didn't speak a word, all the way home.

REPORTING BACK

Dinah dreaded arriving home. All the rest of SPLAT would be there—and so would Ellie. Her mind was full of what had happened at the hospital, and they wouldn't want to talk about anything except DJP.

But when they got home, there was no one in except their mother.

'What's happened?' said Lloyd. 'Aren't the others here?'

'They *were*,' Mrs Hunter said. 'And that girl with the peculiar make-up. But I didn't know when you were going to turn up, so I sent them home. I said you'd ring them when you got in.'

'What about Harvey?' Dinah said. 'Did he go off with them?'

Mrs Hunter shook her head. She looked frazzled. 'I had to send Harvey to the shop. I'm making treacle tarts for the bazaar and I've run out of golden syrup. They didn't have any in the supermarket this morning. And there was a terrible fuss going on. People are getting really sick of these shortages.'

'So *no one*'s here?' Lloyd frowned.

Dinah could see he was feeling frustrated. He wanted a SPLAT meeting straight away. But she didn't.

It would be much better to have one tomorrow—
without Ellie.

She looked round the kitchen. It was full of treacle
tarts with no golden syrup in them. 'Do you want us to
give you a hand, Mum?'

Mrs Hunter looked relieved. 'That would be
wonderful. Otherwise we won't be eating before
midnight.'

Doing things was much easier than talking. While
Lloyd peeled potatoes, Dinah washed up everything she
could find and chopped three onions. By the time she'd
done that, she felt much more relaxed. And Mrs Hunter
was looking happier too. She even laughed at one of
Lloyd's terrible jokes.

It was just as well they'd cheered her up, because
when Harvey came back, his hands were empty.

'I'm sorry,' he said. 'I couldn't find any golden syrup
anywhere. And the supermarket was full of people
yelling at each other. One woman had a go at me. *It's
you young hooligans causing all this upset!* I thought
she was going to hit me with her umbrella.'

'It's all over the papers,' Lloyd said the next day. 'Look at
these.' He picked up a couple of front pages and spread
them out so that everyone in the SPLAT shed could see.

DJ CAUSES UPROAR IN SUPERMARKETS, said
the Hunters' paper.

DJP SPARKS FOOD RIOTS, screamed the one
Mandy had brought.

Mandy pulled a face. 'The whole thing's getting out of hand, isn't it?'

Harvey nodded. 'Mum goes ballistic now every time anyone mentions DJP. *I'd like to get my hands on that man!*'

Ingrid interrupted impatiently. 'Who cares about the stupid newspapers? Ian and I have got something really important to tell you! Something we found out yesterday.'

'You said we were wasting our time yesterday,' Lloyd reminded her.

Ingrid glared at him. 'That was *before*. When we were doing all that stupid hanging around in the High Street. But after that we went back to the shopping mall. And we tracked down the mall administration office.'

'It wasn't easy,' Ian said. 'It's tucked away round the back of the shops.'

'But we found it!' Ingrid said. 'And the man there was quite friendly—'

'—until we started asking him about DJP.' Ian frowned. 'He went really funny then.'

'Let me guess,' said Lloyd. 'He wouldn't say anything except *I am not able to give out any more information about DJ Pardoman.* Right?'

Ingrid's mouth dropped open. 'How did you know that?'

Dinah was watching their faces. *They haven't got it yet*, she thought. *They don't realize.*

Mandy and Harvey were looking startled too. 'B-but that was what *our* man said,' Harvey stuttered. 'In the High Street.'

Lloyd and Dinah didn't answer. They sat very still, letting the others work it out.

Ian got it first. He went pale. 'It's *him*, isn't it? The Headmaster.'

'The Headmaster?' Ingrid said scornfully. 'DJP? You've got to be joking!'

But nobody laughed. She looked round and her scornful grin faded.

'You *believe* it!'

'I wish I didn't,' Mandy said. 'But the unmasking—it's just his sort of thing.'

Harvey looked terrified. 'He's going to hypnotize everyone!'

'No, he's not!' Dinah said. 'Because we're going to stop him!'

She said it without thinking. But the moment the words were out she knew they were true. If DJ Pardoman really was the Headmaster—then he had to be stopped.

'So how are we going to do it?' Ian said. 'We still don't know anything about him, do we?'

Dinah suddenly felt horribly tired. *I don't need this*, she thought. *Not on top of everything else*. But she knew she couldn't back out. The others were all looking at her, waiting for her to make a plan.

'Let's think about the show,' she said slowly. 'It's on in every Purple club in the country, isn't it? At the same time. How does he do that?'

Ingrid shrugged. 'They must broadcast it, like television.'

But Dinah had already thought that one through.

'What we saw wasn't a broadcast. He kept responding to the audience. When they roared, he stopped talking—straight away. And he didn't start again until the noise died down—*just* enough. You can't do that with a broadcast. It's going to be different in every club.'

Lloyd frowned. 'So what are you saying? He can't be live in every club at once. Not unless there are hundreds of different DJPs.'

Dinah shook her head. 'People would have spotted that by now. No, it's the same DJP all right.'

'Everywhere?' Harvey said nervously. 'He's the Headmaster and he's *everywhere*?'

Mandy patted his hand. 'Don't worry. There'll be a simple explanation.' She looked at Dinah. 'How do *you* think he does it?'

'How about some kind of interactive video?' Dinah said.

'You mean—something that can respond to what happens in each club?' Ian nodded slowly. 'It could be.'

Dinah worked it out. 'Some things—when he stops speaking and when he starts again—could be triggered by the noise levels in the club. I'd like to go there again and see if I can spot it happening.'

Mandy looked sheepish. 'Actually—I've already told Ellie we'll be there on Wednesday. She wants to see us all.'

'Don't tell her about the Headmaster!' Dinah said quickly. 'She's such a DJP fan. She'll never believe us.' There was something about Ellie that made her uneasy, but she didn't know what.

Lloyd nodded. 'Di's right. There's no need for Ellie to know what we're thinking. Let her go on thinking we're hunting for DJP because we want to win the competition.'

'I don't care what she thinks,' Ingrid said grimly. 'As long as we find him. I wish it was Wednesday tomorrow, so we could get on with it. Don't you, Di?'

Dinah smiled vaguely, but she didn't say yes. She had other plans for tomorrow. She usually went straight from school to a maths club on Monday evenings. But this Monday she was going to sneak off to the bus station instead.

To catch the five past four bus to Maidborough.

At ten past five on Monday, she was ringing the bell outside Intensive Care. It was Bernadette who opened the door again. She nodded when she saw Dinah.

'We were hoping you'd be back soon. Your father seemed a bit better after you came last time. We think he may have recognized your voice.'

Dinah didn't know what to say to that, but it didn't matter. Bernadette went on talking over her shoulder as she led the way into the ward.

'Could you talk a bit more this time? I know it feels funny—with him not answering—but it might make a difference.'

She fetched a chair and Dinah sat down beside the bed. It was a shock to see the same bandaged face, as blank as before.

'Will he—have to wear those for long?' Dinah tried not to think about what might be underneath.

Bernadette patted her shoulder. 'It's hard, isn't it? Not being able to see him. But he's getting better. Dr Winthrop thought the bandages might have to stay on for another three weeks, but he's talking about taking them off sooner now.'

Oh, I hope he does, Dinah thought. Three weeks seemed a horribly long time. At the moment, all she could really see of Phil Ashby was his hands.

She looked at the fingers lying on the blanket in front of her. They were heavy and strong, with short, clean nails and very white skin. There was nothing at all familiar about them.

Why should there be? she said severely to herself. *Why should you remember fingers that you haven't seen since you were a baby?*

Bernadette smiled. 'You can hold his hand if you like. As long as you're careful with the tubes.'

Slowly Dinah slid her own hand on to the blankets and took hold of Phil Ashby's fingers.

Stupidly, she was expecting them to be ice-cold, like the fingers of a corpse. But they were as warm as her own. They lay loosely in the palm of her hand, not gripping or moving at all. She closed her fingers round them and began to talk, struggling to speak as naturally as possible.

'Hello. I'm hoping you can hear my voice.'

'That's it,' Bernadette said cheerfully. 'Keep it up. And let us know if you see any change. Anything at all.'

Dinah nodded and waited until Bernadette left. Then she began to talk again, just loud enough for the man on the bed to hear—if he could hear anything.

'I know you've never heard my voice before. But I'm hoping I sound like my mother. She was called Sally. Do you remember that name? Sally Glass?'

She paused. There was no sign from the figure on the bed. He went on breathing steadily in and out, his chest rising and falling, his white, swathed head absolutely still. But Dinah had a most curious feeling, as though the eyes behind the bandages were open and staring. Gazing through the whiteness at her, like lights shining through fog.

She started murmuring again. 'What comes into your mind if I say Stephen Glass? Do you recognize that name? Steve Glass?'

Nothing. Just that continual feeling of *attention*. Of someone watching her. She went on speaking the words that came into her head.

'Stephen and Sally. Sally and Steve. Is that familiar? Married when they were both twenty-four. And then there was a baby daughter. Dinah. Dinah Mary Glass.'

She took a breath, wanting him to react to that. But the white face didn't move.

Don't be stupid! Did you expect it to be that easy? She made herself relax, sitting back in the chair.

'I'm called Dinah Hunter now. I've got two adopted brothers—Lloyd and Harvey. We're in a secret society called SPLAT. The Society for the Protection of our Lives Against Them.'

She glanced over her shoulder, but no one else was listening. The other patients were asleep, and the nurses were sitting round their table, gossiping. Dinah let her voice flow on.

'*Them* is all the people the Headmaster gets in his power. He used to be in charge of our school, but he's not a headmaster any more. He just wants to run the whole country.'

It was easy to keep talking about the Headmaster and all his horrible plans.

' . . . last time we thought he'd really gone. He filled his brain with all the knowledge in the world, and it overloaded his mind. But he seems to be back . . . '

She launched into a description of DJ Pardoman and Purple. She was just trying to explain about the supervisor at Sharpley's when a hand tapped her on the shoulder. She jumped so hard that she almost fainted.

It was Bernadette. 'I've been watching him on the screen,' she said. 'It looks as though you're having the same good effect as last time.'

'I've only been talking,' Dinah said.

Bernadette was studying the printout from the monitors. 'Look,' she said. 'He's much steadier when you're here, Dinah. More alert.'

Dinah looked down at the man on the bed. Was it true? Was he really responding to her?

'Can you really hear me?' she said. She squeezed the fingers she was holding.

And faintly—unmistakably—they squeezed back.

The shock of it drained all the blood from Dinah's brain. For a moment she could barely hear or see. When she pulled herself together, Bernadette was staring at her. She had noticed it too.

'I think you'd better talk to Dr Winthrop,' she said.

They called him specially. He came down to the Intensive Care unit and Dinah went into the office to talk to him.

'Well, Miss Ashby,' he said. 'You seem like a pretty important young lady.'

'I'm not—' Dinah started.

But the doctor brushed her words aside, as if she were just being modest. 'What about your mother? Is she here?'

'She died,' Dinah said faintly. 'When I was a baby.'

The doctor nodded and made a note. 'It's obvious that you and your father are very close. When you're here he's much more alert. His blood pressure and his pulse rate are nearly normal and he responds to stimuli. In fact—'

He paused and looked at Dinah, weighing up something in his mind. 'I should tell you,' he said gently, 'that we weren't very hopeful about your father—until you came in. His condition was very serious and he seemed to be sinking.'

'And he's better now?' Dinah said breathlessly.

Dr Winthrop nodded. 'Much better. In fact, I'm thinking about taking off the bandages.'

Dinah closed her eyes for a second. The thought of seeing that hidden face was more of a shock than she'd expected.

'I was thinking of next Monday,' said Dr Winthrop.

Dinah opened her eyes and found him staring at her.

'Are you free then?' he said.

'I—what?' Dinah didn't understand. 'You want me to be here?'

Dr Winthrop nodded. 'It could be very useful. Is there any chance that you could miss a day of school on Monday?'

Dinah walked out of the ward in a daze. She was so stunned that she didn't look at her watch until she was coming out of the hospital. But when she did, she panicked. If she didn't hurry, she was going to miss her bus!

She was ten minutes away from the bus station. She cut it down to seven minutes by running all the way, but she knew she was out of luck as soon as she saw the bus stop. There was no queue. No sign of anyone at all.

And the next bus wasn't until ten o'clock.

There was only one sensible thing to do. Miserably, she pulled out her phone.

Dad? I'm not at the library. I'm in Maidborough . . .

'All right,' Mr Hunter said gently, as his car pulled out

of the bus station. 'You'd better tell me about it. What were you doing in Maidborough?'

It was the moment Dinah had been dreading. She took a deep breath. 'I was visiting someone in the hospital.'

'Yes?' Mr Hunter said. Waiting for more.

'He's in intensive care. Unconscious.'

Mr Hunter's eyebrows went up. 'He?'

Dinah was trying to work out how much she needed to tell. 'He's called Phil Ashby. But that's not his real name. He's lost his memory, you see.'

'And how old is this Phil Ashby?' Mr Hunter said carefully.

Dinah gulped. If he really was Stephen Glass, she knew exactly how old he was. To the day. 'He's a little bit younger than you, I think.'

'I see.' Mr Hunter drew a long breath. 'And how did you meet him?'

'Oh, I've never met him. Except in the hospital. At least—' Dinah broke off.

Mr Hunter took another long breath. They were just coming up to some red traffic lights and he didn't speak until the car had stopped.

Then he said, 'Look, Dinah, just tell me what's going on. I know you're a sensible girl, but everything you say sounds dreadful. Is this some man you've met on the internet?'

Dinah was so surprised that she laughed out loud. 'No, of course it's not!' Then she realized that wasn't quite true. 'Well, sort of, I suppose. I saw his face in a newspaper article on the internet.'

Mr Hunter drew in his breath sharply. Dinah glanced sideways at him and saw his face. She was going to have to tell him. *Don't let him be upset. Please don't let him be upset.*

'It's not like you think,' she said. 'I was hunting for something on the internet. I found Phil Ashby's picture by mistake and I *had* to go and find him. Because he looks—he looks exactly like—' Frantically she hunted for the right words. But there was no easy way to say it. '—I think he's Stephen Glass.'

The traffic lights changed and the car started with a jolt.

'I don't understand,' Mr Hunter said. 'Your father and mother both died in that accident. You know they did.'

'I know,' Dinah said. 'But—look, can you stop somewhere? I'd like to show you the photos.'

Mr Hunter pulled into a slip road in front of some shops and Dinah took the pictures out of her pocket. Switching on the inside light, Mr Hunter studied them carefully.

'It's certainly the same face,' he said. 'But that might not mean anything. It could be a complete coincidence.'

Dinah nodded. 'I know. But I went to Great Ley, to try and find out more about him, and I met the woman he lodges with. She said he lost his memory a bit over ten years ago. He doesn't know who he really is . . .'

Her words trailed away. Mr Hunter was still staring down at the pictures.

'He's in a coma,' Dinah said, in a very small voice.

'They thought he was going to die. But he's better when I'm there. They want me to go back next Monday. When they take the bandages off.'

Mr Hunter sighed. 'If you can help, then you ought to go. But that still doesn't mean he's your father. He might not even be a very nice person.'

'I'll never know, will I?' Dinah said. 'If he doesn't come out of the coma.'

Mr Hunter turned off the inside light and started the car. 'I'll take you into Maidborough on Monday,' he said. 'All right?'

Dinah watched his face as the car pulled out on to the main road. There were hundreds of things she wanted to say, but she wasn't the sort of person who said them.

'Thanks,' she said at last. 'Thanks, Dad.'

Mr Hunter smiled, with his eyes on the road.

SOLD OUT

After school on Wednesday, all six SPLAT members were at the Hunters' house, getting ready for their next visit to Purple. At five o'clock, the doorbell rang and Lloyd went to open it.

Ellie was lounging against the door post, her black-rimmed eyes cold and sharp.

'You've found out something, haven't you?' she said. 'I talked to Mandy on the phone last night and I knew from her voice. But she wouldn't tell me what it was.'

'We're just checking something,' Lloyd said quickly. 'We'll let you know as soon as we're sure.'

'You'd better.' Ellie gave him an icy stare.

Lloyd took a step back and she marched into the house and straight up the stairs, without waiting to be asked.

'Dinah! Mandy!' she called.

Lloyd waited until she was safely out of the way, in Dinah's room, before he went upstairs himself. This time he was going to be properly dressed for Purple—but he didn't want any help. Especially not from Ellie.

When he'd finished dressing, he stood for a moment,

admiring his reflection in the mirror. He'd pinned rows of badges across the front of an old T-shirt and added a bright green belt to his ancient jeans. Then he'd spiked his hair up with green hair gel. *Not bad*, he thought.

But if he was expecting any praise, he was disappointed. When he went downstairs, the others were huddled in the kitchen, trying to calm Ingrid down.

'It's a disaster!' she was saying. 'It's ruined everything! We can't go now!'

Ellie was looking angry. 'I *told* you what to bring! How could you forget?'

'What's the matter?' said Lloyd.

Ingrid gave a great wail. 'We need some golden syrup! And your mum hasn't got any.'

'It'll be all right,' Harvey said. 'We'll just have to do without.'

Ingrid wailed again. 'But we won't be able to join in at the end!'

'Don't go crazy,' Lloyd said. 'We'll try and get some at the supermarket.'

Dinah nodded. 'Don't worry, Ing. I'll go with you.'

But Ingrid couldn't stop worrying. When they got on the bus, she refused to sit down. She insisted on standing by the doors, ready to leap off at the earliest possible moment.

Lloyd and Dinah stood with her, but it wasn't a comfortable place to be. Everyone else knew exactly why they were standing there and voices jeered at them, all the way.

'In a *sticky* position, are you?'

'Missed a *golden* opportunity?'

'Sweet enough on your own, then?'

Mandy kept smiling sympathetically at them, but Harvey and Ian looked awkward and Ellie was furious.

'You'd better get to the club in time,' she muttered. She glared at them and went right down to the far end of the bus, pretending not to know them.

Lloyd turned his back on the jeerers. 'Just ignore them,' he muttered to Ingrid.

'We'll soon have some golden syrup of our own,' said Dinah.

'We'd *better*!' Ingrid said.

The moment they reached their stop, she was away, jumping off the bus and racing towards the supermarket. Dinah and Lloyd followed her, and loud shouts and cheers came from the rest of the bus.

'Goin' for *gold*, are you?'

'*Stick* at it!'

'Hope they sell you twenty tins!'

Not much chance of *that*! As soon as he got off the bus, Lloyd saw the big crowd in the supermarket doorway. People were yelling and arguing and both the revolving doors were jammed.

But Ingrid didn't stop running. There were other feet pounding behind them, but she stayed in front all the way—or almost all the way.

Just before she reached the edge of the crowd, she flagged suddenly. Coming up behind her, Lloyd saw the huge notice that filled one of the big shop windows.

NO SYRUP. SORRY.

Lloyd and Dinah slowed down as well, but the two boys behind them swept straight past. They were moving so fast that they ploughed straight into the crowd. Two teenage girls shrieked and punched them and a tall man grabbed them by their collars.

Lloyd tried to pull Ingrid away, but she hissed angrily at him.

'Leave me alone! I want to see what happens.'

The tall man was bellowing at the two boys. 'Get out of here, you! We don't want any more of your sort here, causing trouble!'

The boys were shouting too.

'What's your problem, grandpa?'

'It's not a crime to go shopping!'

They were struggling to get free, but before they could break his grip the crowd parted suddenly. A security man came marching out of the shop, with a line of shop assistants behind him.

He looked the boys up and down and glanced past them, at Lloyd and Dinah and Ingrid and the other teenagers in the crowd.

'Let's not have any trouble,' he said. 'There's no point in you lot coming in here. Can't you see the notice? We haven't got a tin of golden syrup in the place. Sold out two days ago.'

'So?' one of the boys said aggressively. 'Didn't you get some more then?'

The security man sighed impatiently. 'Where from? The warehouses have run out too.'

The other boy put his fists up. 'Yeah? Expect us to believe that?'

The crowd rumbled angrily and the security man sighed again. 'You kids don't realize the trouble you're causing. When you all decide to buy something, it sells out, all over the country. Why can't you give people some warning about what you want?'

'But that's the *game*!' said one of the girls in the crowd. 'Don't you get it? The message comes out of nowhere and you have to be clued up and act fast to be in on it.'

'May be fun for you,' the security man said bitterly. 'But it's doing this store a lot of damage. The ordering system's gone haywire. It's ordered tons of bananas because you bought so many last week. And they're just sitting there rotting. Can't you take those instead?'

'Don't be stupid!' the first boy said rudely. 'Bananas aren't any use.' He had wriggled free of the tall man's grip now and he began to advance on the security man. 'It's golden syrup we want. And I bet you've got some hidden away somewhere!'

All the teenagers in the crowd began to move too, pushing the older people out of the way and heading for the supermarket doorway. Lloyd glanced at Dinah and she nodded quickly.

'We're better off out of here,' she murmured. 'We're not going to get any syrup—and it's nearly time for Purple to open.'

Ingrid pulled a face, but she nodded and began to edge backwards, away from the shop.

The moment the three of them were clear of the crowd, they started to run. But they'd left it too late. They could already hear the crowd outside Purple beginning the countdown.

'TEN! NINE! EIGHT! . . . '

'Quick!' Ingrid swung round the corner of the supermarket and threw herself at the back of the crowd. People were knocked aside by the force of the impact.

'She shouldn't—' Dinah panted.

'Well, she is!' Lloyd said sharply. 'So we've got to keep up with her!'

They raced after her, before the gap closed. The chanting was just finishing, and Ingrid was still running, desperate to make it to the front of the crowd.

' . . . FOUR! THREE! TWO! ONE!—ZERO!'

There was a yell of triumph. The silver shutter began to slide up and Ingrid lowered her head, butting people out of her way. By the time the shutter was fully raised, she was only a few metres from the entrance doors, with Lloyd and Dinah close behind her.

Ellie was just ahead of them, with the others. She glanced back and saw Ingrid and a flash of relief crossed her face. For a moment, Lloyd thought all of them would make it into the club.

But he had reckoned without the heavies. When Ingrid finally reached the arches, two huge pairs of arms shot out towards her. She struggled and screamed, but it was no use. The heavies lifted her high into the air and tossed her into the crowd. The people she had pushed aside grabbed her gleefully and passed her back over their heads.

Dinah turned round. 'I'll have to go and find her!' she yelled. 'She can't stay out here on her own!'

Lloyd turned too.

Dinah shook her head at him. 'No point in both of us missing it! Get in there—and WATCH!'

Then she was gone and Lloyd was swept on towards the arch, fumbling in his pocket to get his money out. When he was through, he looked round to find out what had happened to Dinah and Ingrid, but he couldn't even see them. They were hidden by the wall of people pressing on into the club.

11

MEDIAJAM

By the time Dinah reached the back of the crowd, she was breathless and exhausted from struggling in the wrong direction. But as she reached Ingrid, the movement stopped. From inside the club a loud voice boomed over their heads.

'You people outside are UNlucky today. Stand clear of the shutter.'

There was a moan from the crowd and the silver shutter began to slide down. Dinah could almost taste the disappointment in the air.

Ingrid was furious. She clenched her fists. 'It's not fair! It's not *fair*! Those heavies have ruined everything. And they really hurt!'

There were red marks on her arms where the heavies had seized her.

'What do you expect?' Dinah said. 'If they're working for the Headmaster, they'll do whatever he's told them to. Like machines. They won't care how you feel.'

Ingrid scowled. 'Well, he's not going to beat us!'

She stood on tiptoe, peering over the shoulders of the people in front of them to see what was happening. Everyone was shuffling sideways, spreading out to leave a clear space in front of the closed shutter.

And people were taking out their tins of golden syrup.

'What d'you think they're going to do?' Ingrid whispered. 'Spread it all over the ground?'

Dinah imagined it. 'Sounds sticky.'

A boy stepped into the central space, holding an open tin of syrup. He lifted it high and tilted it, ready to pour. But the rest of the crowd groaned and began to chant aggressively.

'Dull! Dull! Dull!'

The boy grinned. Then he swung the tin over his head and turned it upside down. A thick dollop of syrup fell slowly on to his head. Dropping the tin, he began to smear the syrup down his hair and over his face.

The crowd cheered and a girl jumped out of it to stand beside him. She had a crumpled piece of newspaper in her hand. She ripped it up and pressed the bits on to the syrup and they stuck there, flapping at the edges.

It was like a signal. Immediately, everyone began to move. People came forward with more syrup and more pieces of paper—bus tickets, tissues, flyers for Purple. Whatever they had in their pockets was torn up and pressed on, until the boy who had started it all was completely covered. He strutted about like a strange bird with pale feathers flapping.

'Hey, that's really funny!' Ingrid said.

She started forward, to join in, but she found herself facing a line of girls with white faces and purple lipstick. Dinah hadn't been expecting to see any First Purples outside, but there were five of them and they glared at

Ingrid with black-rimmed eyes, freezing her where she stood.

'Where's your syrup?' one of them said roughly.

Ingrid clenched her fists and Dinah answered quickly, before things could get worse.

'We forgot it. And when we asked in the shop—'

But the girls weren't interested in explanations.

'No free-loaders!' they chanted. And they began to march forward.

Dinah didn't wait to argue. She grabbed Ingrid's hand and dragged her away, towards the Purple building. She didn't stop until they were right round at the side, behind the dustbins.

Ingrid muttered rebelliously, but she stayed there until the coast was clear. Then she and Dinah peered round the corner again.

Everyone seemed to be getting as sticky as possible. A group of girls had smeared themselves with syrup and they were rolling in a heap of dry leaves at one side of the car park. When they danced back into the central space, their bodies were brown and rustling.

Other people were hunting for things to stick on to themselves. Three boys charged round to the side of the building where Dinah and Ingrid were hiding. Tipping over the wheelie bins, they started scavenging through the rubbish, pulling out letters and old envelopes and bits of cardboard to rip up and press on to their bodies.

Everybody seemed to be covered in syrup. Boys were running round, bumping into each other and squelching apart. Girls were pulling their hair into fantastic syrupy peaks, or twisting it into tight buns, slicked close to their heads. And three people were tipping syrup over the cars on the far side of the car park. When the bodywork was covered, they clambered on to the roofs and rolled down the bonnets.

Dinah shuddered. It was chaos. She and Ingrid edged forward, still keeping in the shadow of the Purple building. They had to pick their way carefully, because the ground was spattered with syrup and littered with debris from the overturned rubbish bins.

Everything that wasn't suitable for sticking on had been dropped or kicked aside. Old pieces of pizza and aluminium cans. A comb and a kettle. An empty printer cartridge. Most of the paper had been torn up, but there was plenty of rubbish left over. A plastic noodle pot. An old box file. A padded envelope.

Dinah stepped straight over the padded envelope before the word on the label caught her eye. *Purple*. She turned round and picked it up.

'Yuck!' said Ingrid. 'How *can* you?'

The envelope was covered in syrup and there were little stones and pieces of dirt stuck all over the underside.

'It might be important,' Dinah said. She ripped the label off the front of the envelope and dropped the rest of it.

Immediately, a girl raced over and snatched it up. It was leaking grey fluff now, and she began to empty out the fluff with cries of excitement, smearing her sticky face with it until she looked like a grey cat. Then she pranced off into the crowd, purring loudly.

Dinah shook her head. 'They've all gone wild.'

'We'd be doing it too,' Ingrid said. 'If we had any syrup. It's more fun than collecting litter for nothing.' She leaned over and looked at the label in Dinah's hand. 'What's so great about that anyway? There's nothing on it except the club's address. And we know that already.'

But Dinah had read the label more carefully. She pointed to the top of it, where the return address was printed. 'Look where it's come from.'

Ingrid peered at the postmark. 'London?'

'Not that! *Look!*' Dinah ran her finger along the address. *MediaJam, 624 Conal Street, London LO4 9QT.*

'So?' Ingrid said.

Dinah glanced round. She didn't want anyone to overhear. Leaning closer to Ingrid, she tapped the code letters printed in the left-hand corner of the address label. *P137 WK 19.*

'What do you think that means?'

'How should I know?' Ingrid said. 'I hate guessing games.'

'I'll tell you what I think,' Dinah said. 'I think it means *Purple 137, Week 19.* Whatever was in this parcel was sent to all the other Purple clubs too. And it's something that gets sent every week.'

Ingrid looked blank. 'Like what?' She was blowing on her hands and stamping her feet up and down and she had started to shiver.

Dinah looked at her. Then she looked at her watch. It was over two hours until the others would come out of the club.

'There's a café next to the supermarket,' she said. 'Why don't we go in there? We could have a warm drink and try to work things out.'

'Good idea.' Ingrid looked relieved.

She didn't say anything else until they were sitting down in the café, but she must have been thinking. As she curled her fingers round her mug of hot chocolate, she said, 'You think that packet had this week's programme in. Don't you?'

Thank goodness she's worked it out too. Dinah nodded. 'I think the whole show comes through the post on a DVD, every week.' She flapped the label. 'From here.'

Ingrid stared at the address. 'You think we'll find the Headmaster if we go there?'

'We might,' Dinah said. 'We'll certainly find out *something.*'

'Could be dangerous.' Ingrid took a quick sip of her hot chocolate, still looking thoughtfully at the address.

They were on their third mug of chocolate when the café staff began to put the chairs up on the tables and mop the floor. They stared at Dinah and Ingrid, working their way closer and closer to where they were sitting.

'We'd better go before they throw us out,' Dinah said. 'The others will be out in half an hour anyway.'

'Ready to be covered in golden syrup.' Ingrid pulled a face. 'I hope they think of something better to bring next week.'

There was someone by their table now, tapping her foot impatiently. Dinah stood up. 'Come on.'

But Ingrid was still thinking. 'Who decides what people have to bring, anyway? And how does everyone find out?'

Dinah wasn't really listening. 'It's probably just one of those things,' she said vaguely. 'Now hurry up, before they throw us out.'

'But—'

'No, come *on*!' Dinah put a hand in between Ingrid's shoulder blades and pushed her into the rotating door. 'Let's go and find the others.' She hardly noticed that Ingrid was still talking.

' . . . and do you think they get people to bring the same thing to all the Purple clubs . . . ?'

Dinah meant to tell Lloyd about MediaJam straight away. But he didn't let her get a word in edgeways. He was full of what he'd noticed inside the club.

'You were absolutely right, Di. No doubt about it. The video—or whatever it is—responds to noise. They have a sort of bridge section when DJP isn't doing anything much. Just listening, with his head on one side. And the moment the noise goes up—or down—enough, the video switches to the next thing. It's done really cleverly, so there's no awkward jump.

But it sticks out a mile once you know what to look for . . .'

It obviously didn't occur to him that Dinah and Ingrid might have discovered something too. And before Dinah could get him to listen, Ellie had raced up, sticky with golden syrup and covered with glittering, rustling crisp packets.

She looked sharply at Dinah. 'What did you and Ingrid do? While the rest of us were in the club?'

'We went in the café,' Dinah said. Very fast, before Ingrid could give anything else away. 'It was cold out here, so we went and had some hot chocolate.'

Ellie stared at her for a moment and then went swooping off again.

'Don't try and tell the others now,' Dinah hissed in Ingrid's ear. 'We'll wait for the SPLAT meeting. There's bound to be one tomorrow.'

She was right. They met straight after school. But even then it was difficult to get Lloyd to believe that she and Ingrid had some news.

'You were only in the car park!' he said.

'We keep our eyes open!' said Ingrid. 'Even in car parks! And you'd better listen to us—because we've found out where they make those videos of DJP!'

'We *think* we've found out,' Dinah said, more cautiously. 'We found a padded envelope with an address in London and some kind of number code.'

She held out the label she had torn off the envelope

and Lloyd took it. Ian and Harvey and Mandy crowded round to see.

'It's just a guess,' Dinah said. 'But I'm sure we're right. Only—I don't know how to check.'

Mandy looked up. 'We could—' she said. And stopped.

'Go on,' said Ian. 'Spit it out.'

Mandy went pink. 'I know it sounds like a stupid suggestion, but if this place is a recording studio we could try and—book it.'

'*What?*' said Lloyd.

Mandy went even pinker. 'I could phone up and pretend I wanted to book it. And that would give me an excuse to ask questions.'

'But they won't waste time talking to a kid,' said Ian.

'They don't have to know I'm a kid.' Mandy grinned. 'Haven't you ever heard me imitate my Auntie Emma?' She cleared her throat and put on a very solemn expression. When she spoke again, her voice came out a whole tone deeper. She sounded very confident. 'Good morning. Amanda Rothwell here. I'm the manager of the Shooting Stars.'

Ingrid and Harvey giggled, but Lloyd looked impressed. 'Hey, that's great! You really do sound grown-up.'

'Shall I do it, then?' Mandy pulled out her phone.

'Hang on a minute,' said Dinah. 'You need to sort out what you're going to say first.'

Ian nodded. 'You ought to ask about when it's free. And what it costs—'

'And what the studios are like,' Ingrid chipped in. 'And if you've got to bring a script and a producer—'

Mandy put her hands over her ears. 'I can't remember all that. I'll get in a muddle and sound stupid.'

Lloyd was making notes. 'You can look at these if you get stuck. You ought to try and find out what day they film the Purple video as well.'

'Don't be silly!' Ingrid said scornfully. 'She can't ask *that*!'

'Maybe she doesn't need to,' Dinah said slowly. She'd been thinking about the timing. 'I reckon they have to film it on Saturdays—if the studio's open then. Or Mondays at the latest.'

'Why not earlier?' said Harvey.

Dinah shrugged. 'Can't be before Friday evening. He knows what's top of the charts, doesn't he?'

'That's true,' Lloyd said. 'And if it's later, they wouldn't have time to edit the video and send out the DVDs by Wednesday.'

'If we can find out when they do the recording, we can go there!' Harvey said eagerly. 'And see if DJP really is the Headmaster?'

Dinah had a sudden, frightening picture of Harvey surrounded by tall men with blank eyes and cruel hands.

'We need to be careful,' she said. 'If DJP really *is* the Headmaster, he'll have everyone round him under his control. Agents and sound engineers and producers— they'll all be hypnotized.'

'He can't hypnotize *us*, though,' said Ian.

'Except for me.' Dinah looked away.

Everyone else in SPLAT was immune to hypnotism, but she wasn't. She knew how horrible it was. And she didn't want to go through that again. The terrible, crooning voice . . .

You are feeling sleepy, Dinah. So, so sleepy . . .

And then—nothing. No consciousness of what happened next. No memory of the Headmaster's instructions. Just a blank in her mind—and lies coming out of her mouth before she knew what she was saying.

She looked up again and met Lloyd's eyes.

'We've got to try everything,' he said. And she knew he was right.

Mandy nodded. 'Just wait while I find the phone number.'

And, in minutes, it was all set up. Mandy put on her Aunt-Emma face and dialled the studio while Lloyd frowned at the others, trying keep them quiet.

'Good afternoon,' Mandy said solemnly. 'My name is Amanda Rothwell. I'm the manager of the Shooting Stars—'

That was when Ingrid started to giggle.

She went bright red and pressed her lips together, but she couldn't stop—and Lloyd wasn't taking any chances. He and Dinah launched themselves at her, jamming their hands over her mouth and pulling her over to the other side of the shed.

'I'm looking for somewhere to make a promotional video,' Mandy went on, sounding quite unruffled. 'And I wondered what kind of facilities you have—' Ingrid snorted and struggled, but Lloyd and Dinah held on tight. They couldn't let her laugh. If the phone picked that up, it would give everything away.

' . . . expecting to be in the area on Saturday through to Monday,' Mandy was saying. 'I wonder if it would be possible . . . '

Harvey was grinning and biting his lip now. And even Dinah was struggling to stay quiet. It was hilarious hearing Mandy sound so businesslike.

' . . . no, I'm sorry.' Her voice was very firm. 'I have to be in Leeds on Tuesday. And I'm flying to New York on Wednesday. If you really haven't got five minutes to talk to a client . . . '

Lloyd freed one hand from Ingrid and clapped it over his own mouth, and Ian pressed his arm against his face. None of them could take in what Mandy was saying. They were just concentrating on staying silent until she'd finished.

The moment she switched the phone off, they went into storms of laughter, rolling round the shed and shaking helplessly.

Mandy shook her head at them. 'You're hopeless!'

'You were fantastic, Mandy!' Lloyd gasped. 'You sounded about forty.'

Ingrid was still giggling. 'Did they take you seriously?'

'They certainly did,' Mandy said. 'I've made an appointment to look at the studio. Next Monday. Because they're closed on Saturdays.'

That stopped them laughing. They all stared at her, working out what that meant.

Mandy waited until they were absolutely silent. Then she said, 'I have to be there early, because the place is booked from midday.' She paused. 'It's a regular booking they have every Monday.'

There was a long, nervous pause. Then Lloyd said, 'Well, it looks as though we'll all be skipping school then.'

And that was when Dinah remembered where she'd promised to be on Monday.

12

WITHOUT DINAH

'What?' Lloyd said. 'What do you mean you're not coming?'

Dinah had caught him on his own, on Saturday morning, and he couldn't believe what she was telling him.

'I've got to be at the hospital on Monday,' Dinah said miserably. 'They're going to take his bandages off. The doctor wants me there and Mum and Dad said I could miss school. Because it's so important.'

'More important than the Headmaster?' Lloyd said furiously. 'You don't think he matters any more?'

'Of course he matters,' said Dinah. 'It's just—'

Lloyd finished the sentence for her. 'It's just that Phil Ashby matters more? The Headmaster may be a threat to the whole country, but that's not important, is it?'

'Yes it is!' Dinah said. 'It *is*! But the doctor asked me specially. And I promised.'

'Oh well,' said Lloyd sarcastically. 'If you *promised*.'

He knew he was being unfair, but he couldn't help it. He wanted Dinah to come to London. They needed her.

'What am I going to tell the others?' he said. 'Or don't you care about them either?'

'Of course I care about them!' Dinah was almost in tears now. 'But *I have to go to the hospital*.'

'Go to the hospital then!' Lloyd glared at her. 'And if the rest of us get into trouble for skipping school *without* permission—well, you'll be nice and safe, won't you?' He stamped out of the room.

He couldn't warn Harvey, because he'd promised not to tell him about Phil Ashby. So on Monday morning, Harvey was taken completely by surprise. He and Lloyd came down in uniform, as usual, pretending they were off to school. When Dinah appeared at breakfast in jeans and a sweatshirt, Harvey was baffled. He looked up from his plate of toast and his mouth dropped open.

'Leave her alone,' Mrs Hunter said, before he could ask anything. 'She'll tell you all about it when she's ready.'

Lloyd finished his orange juice and stood up. 'Come on, Harvey,' he said loudly. 'We don't want to be late. The others will be waiting.'

Looking bewildered, Harvey swallowed his last mouthful of toast. 'Hang on. I've got to find my shoes.'

Lloyd stood by the front door, looking impatiently at his watch. He couldn't say, *Hurry up or we'll miss our train*, but he hoped Harvey knew how little time there was.

He did. He came scuttling down the stairs with his shoelaces flapping, crouched at the bottom to tie them and snatched up his bag and his coat.

'Why isn't Di coming?' he whispered.

'Because she's not!' Lloyd snapped. 'Now let's get going.'

He opened the door and they both shot through it, with Harvey pulling on his coat as they went. Ian and Mandy and Ingrid were at the corner already, watching anxiously for them.

'At last!' Ingrid said. 'Where's Dinah?'

'Not coming,' Lloyd said.

He was tight-lipped and furious and they walked to the station in silence.

It looked easy in the London *A to Z*. Two tube trains from the main-line station and then a short walk to Conal Street.

It was longer in real life and it was an hour before they finally turned into Conal Street. They were already late for the appointment.

They found themselves in a narrow, bleak road, with tall old buildings on each side. The dirty yellow bricks seemed to swallow the light, making it sour and dingy, and the buildings turned blank faces to the street.

Lloyd was expecting a big, imposing film studio with a huge sign across the front and glass doors opening into a glittering foyer. But there was nothing like that. All the buildings had wooden doors with dozens of little nameplates covering the wall on either side of the doorway. They were nearly at the end before they found the right one.

'It's here!' Ingrid squealed.

'SSSSH!!!' The others all said it together.

Ingrid pulled a face and said it again, in a loud whisper, pointing. '*It's here!*'

She was right. The name was second from the top on the right-hand side. *MediaJam—4H*. There was an entryphone beside the bell, and a security camera above the door.

Lloyd looked at it. 'Well?' he said. 'Are you ready, Mandy? You're the one who's got to get us inside.'

Mandy took a deep breath. She was very nervous, but she looked fantastic. Ingrid had spent hours getting her ready. She had combed Mandy's long red hair forward over one shoulder and back over the other and made her wear Harvey's cap, tilting it forward so that her face was shadowed.

'You need something to hold,' Ingrid said. She looked round and grabbed the folder that Lloyd was holding. 'That's it. Now pretend to be grown-up.'

Mandy frowned for a moment, and then stood up very straight, like a ruler. Ingrid rolled her eyes and pulled a face.

'That's hopeless! They'll think you're really weird if you look like that. Can't you be more laid back? You're supposed to be in the music industry.'

Mandy slumped, slouching forward and holding the folder over her stomach.

'That's worse,' Ingrid said impatiently. 'You're just not getting it. I think I ought to do it instead. I'd be brilliant.'

Mandy looked miserable. 'You *would* be much better than me. Maybe you ought to try—'

'She's too short,' Lloyd said. 'It's got to be you, Mandy.'

'But I *can't*.' Mandy looked even more miserable.

'Why don't you pretend to be someone else?' Harvey said. 'Pretend to be Ingrid.'

Ingrid gave an indignant splutter, but Mandy grinned suddenly.

Cheekily.

She stood up straight in quite a different way, with her weight on one leg and her chin lifted boldly. Tucking the folder jauntily under her arm, she looked curiously from side to side, tilting her head and tapping a foot.

Ingrid was outraged. 'I don't look like that!'

But the others were all grinning.

'That's wonderful,' Lloyd said. 'Let's go for it.'

Mandy swung into the porch. The others flattened themselves against the front of the building, out of range of the security camera. When she was sure that they couldn't be seen, Mandy rang the bell.

The entryphone crackled. 'MediaJam,' said a man's voice.

Mandy smiled and spoke into it in her Aunt-Emma voice. 'Amanda Rothwell to see Keith Dyett.'

The entryphone crackled again, saying something Lloyd couldn't catch. Then the door lock buzzed. Mandy pushed it open quickly, stepped inside and held it for the others.

'Not yet!' Lloyd hissed. 'Wait a minute, until they've stopped looking at the camera picture.'

He counted to ten and then signalled that they could go. One by one, they slid round the corner and into the building.

Gently, Mandy closed the door. 'He said we can only have a few minutes. The people who've booked the session are already there. They're in the dressing room getting ready.'

'You mean—*he's* there?' Lloyd felt as though someone had punched him hard in the stomach. If they were right about DJ Pardoman, the Headmaster was there. Now. In the same building as they were.

'We've got to try and find him,' Ian said softly.

'We can pretend to be the Shooting Stars,' said Ingrid. 'We can all burst in together—'

Harvey frowned. 'But no one will believe us.'

'Doesn't matter.' Ian was already pressing the lift button. 'We've only got to distract them for a minute. While we find the dressing room.'

Lloyd glanced sideways at Harvey as they got into the lift.

'Don't come in with us,' he said. 'There's got to be someone who knows where we've gone. Hang back and watch.'

Harvey nodded. Suddenly he was very pale.

They stepped out of the lift into a corridor that twisted left and then right. After the second corner, there were two blank doors facing each other, one on either side of the corridor. Beyond them, at the far end, was the MediaJam office, looking back down the corridor.

'OK everyone,' Lloyd muttered. 'Here we go.' He looked at Harvey. 'If it looks as though things are going wrong—leg it out of the building and phone the police.'

Harvey shrank back, out of sight. Lloyd nodded at Mandy and she pushed the office door open and burst in.

'Good morning! I'm Amanda Rothwell—and I've brought the band with me.'

Ingrid was close behind, grinning enthusiastically. 'It's Lloyd on keyboard and Ian on vocals, and I'm the drummer!'

The only person in the office was a young man sitting with his feet on the desk, talking on the phone. He blinked when he saw Mandy. When the others appeared he frowned and stood up quickly.

'I'll call you back,' he said into the phone. 'Something's come up.'

He switched off and put the phone down.

'What's going on?' he said furiously. 'You're just a load of kids!'

'What's wrong with kids?' Ingrid snapped back. 'Don't you like our music?'

The young man stood up. 'This isn't a youth club. We're running a serious business and we've got a lot of work to get through today. Go away—before I call the police.'

Lloyd looked round frantically. He'd been expecting to see other rooms opening off the office. A studio and a dressing room at least. But there was nothing. The office looked straight over the back yard.

There was only one thing to do. Lloyd stood very straight and looked the man in the eye. 'OK,' he said. 'So we're not a band. But we've got a good reason to be here. We've taken up DJ Pardoman's challenge to find out about him—and we've tracked him down to this building. We know he's here. And we want to see him.'

For a moment, he thought the man was going to faint. He stopped dead and his face went white. Then he reached backward and pressed a button on the phone.

The phone buzzed. 'Ready to start?' said a voice. 'About time.'

'Trouble,' said the young man. 'We've got some kids here saying they want to see DJP.'

There was no answer. But a split second later, there was a rush of feet behind Lloyd. Three huge men wearing purple tracksuits came rushing into the room. They looked like warthogs in trainers.

'OK, kids,' one of them said. 'We want you out of here in thirty seconds.'

Lloyd raised his hands. There was one more thing to try, but he had to be out in the corridor for that. Without any heavies hanging on to him. 'Don't worry,' he said. 'We'll go.'

Ingrid was horrified. 'You're not giving in?'

'There's nothing we can do, Ing.' Mandy put an arm round her shoulders.

'That's right.' Lloyd looked round at them all. Then, very deliberately, he said, 'Come on, SPLAT.'

They never used that name when anyone else could hear them. He hoped they would understand the signal and guess that he had a plan.

One of the heavies opened the door and waved them through. Lloyd shrugged, looking as miserable as he could. He walked out of the office, glancing down the corridor towards the two blank doors. One on the left and one on the right.

One of them *had* to be the dressing room. Harvey would know which one, if he'd seen the heavies race through it—but where was Harvey? Without him there was only a fifty-fifty chance of getting the right door.

The heavies fell into step around them, watching them all the time. They were obviously set to escort them out of the building. Lloyd sighed dramatically. 'Well, that's it,' he said. Loud enough for Harvey to hear if he was anywhere around. 'We did the best we could, but we've failed.'

Behind him, Mandy sighed too. And Ian scuffed his feet sulkily along the floor. *Any minute now*, Lloyd was thinking. *Any minute now, I'll just have to guess and choose one of the doors. If I guess wrong, it's just too bad. There won't be a second chance.*

But at the very last moment, when they were almost past the doors, Harvey's face suddenly peered anxiously round the corner.

Lloyd raised his eyebrows, glancing left and right at the two doors, and Harvey understood straight away. He nodded quickly at the door on Lloyd's right. Then he stepped out into the middle of the corridor, so that the heavies could see him properly.

'Not another kid!' one of them said. 'Oi! Come here, you!'

Harvey stuck out his tongue and then turned round and ran. Immediately, in an automatic reaction, the heavies all started forward. They only took a couple of steps, but it gave Lloyd the chance he needed. He darted sideways and wrenched open the door on his right.

And there was DJ Pardoman.

He was leaning back in a chair, with his feet on the dressing table. As the door opened, he turned to see who was coming in, and Lloyd found himself staring straight into the face of Winston Churchill, complete with cigar.

He didn't hesitate. Launching himself into the room, he grabbed the mask with both hands. For a second he couldn't move it. Then he found the catch at the back and flicked it open. Before the man in the chair could react, he had wrenched the mask upwards, tearing it off.

'. . . A CHANCE TO SEE HIS FACE . . .'

Dinah was looking down at the bandages that covered Phil Ashby's face.

'It was dreadful,' she said. 'Lloyd was furious. He didn't understand why I had to be here.'

The muffled face was completely motionless, but Dinah was sure he could hear her. When she spoke, his stillness seemed to grow stiller, more like attention than unconsciousness. She could feel a link between them, a thread holding them together.

'I want to be here,' she said. 'But I want to be with SPLAT too, because they're my friends. They've gone off to London to find DJ Pardoman—and we think he's the Headmaster. So they could be in danger. I just wish—'

I wish I could be in two places at once.

The man on the bed shifted slightly, his fingers tightening round hers. Dinah scribbled a note with her free hand.

11.05 a.m. Weak squeeze.

'Very good,' said Bernadette when she came to look. 'Keep it up. Dr Winthrop will be round in an hour or so.'

'Will he take the bandages off then?' Dinah said eagerly.

Bernadette laughed. 'Not quite then. He'll probably want another EEG, to check that your dad's condition is steady.'

'And *then* he'll do it?'

'I think so.' Bernadette smiled. 'Some time this afternoon, I expect. You keep up what you're doing and things will be fine.'

It was nearly one o'clock when the doctor finally appeared. He beamed at Dinah, looked at Phil Ashby's notes and beamed again.

'Well, you seem to be doing a good job. Have you been here long?'

'I got here just after nine,' Dinah said.

Dr Winthrop looked at his watch. 'You must be ready for a break. Why don't you run down to the café while we're examining your father?'

'That's a good idea.' Bernadette nodded. 'I'm sure you could do with some lunch. Know where the café is?'

'I'll find it.' Dinah grinned and headed out of the ward. Talking all the time was thirsty work. And Bernadette was right. She was hungry.

The café was down on the next floor. It was called *C U There*. Dinah pulled a face at the name and pushed the door open.

Someone inside was very angry.

'So what am I supposed to do?' bellowed a voice. 'How can I manage without eggs? *Give them something else*, everyone says. Hah! Let them try catering for a hospital with no eggs. The chef's going ballistic. He's threatening to resign. And where will I be then?'

Dinah went in. A huge woman, like a tank, was leaning on the counter in front of her, moaning to the man at the till. Behind her, half a dozen other customers were shuffling impatiently, balancing their trays on the rail.

'This week it's eggs,' the woman rumbled. 'Last week it was golden syrup, and before that it was bananas. What's it going to be next week? Potatoes? Milk? Teabags? Why doesn't the government *take charge*?'

She was tense and upset as well as angry. Someone behind her muttered something about moving on, and she turned round and exploded.

'Why does everyone have to be so impatient? Can't you see I've got a problem here? I'm responsible for feeding every single person in this hospital AND I'M GOING OUT OF MY MIND!'

The whole queue took a step back, away from her. The only one who dared to reply was a small woman immediately in front of Dinah. She was a middle-aged, meek-and-mild sort of woman, with grey hair and a beige dress, and she mumbled something, without lifting her head.

' . . . might be all right after Wednesday.'

'What's that?' The big woman turned and strode down the line. For one wild moment, Dinah thought she was actually going to pick the small one up and shake her. 'Did you say something? Do you think you can do my job better than I can? Do *you* want to do the catering here?'

The small woman shook her head hastily. ' . . . only said . . . '

'SPEAK UP!' the huge woman bellowed.

The small one looked as if she might faint. She coughed again and raised her voice. 'I just said—it might be all right after Wednesday. Once they've seen his face, the whole thing might die down.'

The big woman clenched her fists, threateningly. 'What are you talking about?'

Two or three other people in the queue suddenly found their voices.

' . . . it's those Purple clubs . . . '

' . . . happens all over the country . . . '

' . . . the kids are so crazy about DJ Pardoman . . . '

'DJ?' The big woman's mouth fell open and her eyebrows went up high. 'You're telling me all these shortages are caused by some DJ?'

Everyone in the queue nodded vigorously.

'Just let me get my hands on him!' The big woman bared her teeth. 'What does he look like?'

More babble.

The big woman frowned. Dinah could see she was just about to lose her temper again. But before that happened, a tall man spoke up clearly, from the front of the queue.

'That's just the point. No one knows what he looks like. But we'll know soon, because he's going to be unmasked on Wednesday. On television. That'll give everyone a chance to see his face!'

The big woman smiled suddenly, baring her teeth. 'I'll be watching!' she said.

'Me too!' said the little grey-haired woman in front of Dinah.

Everyone felt the same.

' . . . can't wait to see what he looks like . . . '

' . . . he won't dare go out when everyone knows . . . '

' . . . have to have plastic surgery to change his face . . . '

'It's obviously going to be the most popular news programme ever,' said the tall man with a grin. 'Looks as though the whole country will be watching.'

Everyone laughed—except for Dinah. She stood at the back of the queue and shuddered. If the whole country was watching, who would escape the Headmaster's eyes? They would all stare into the sea-green eyes behind the mask and hear the steady, crooning voice.

You must all be very tired after the trouble you've been having at the shops. You must be so-o-o-o tired and sleepy . . .

That was all it would take—and the whole country would be changed for ever. The Headmaster would take over and start to run things his way.

The big woman had calmed down now and gone off to drink her coffee and the queue was moving at last. But when Dinah reached the front, she found that she'd lost her appetite.

Ordering a lemonade, she went to sit by the window. She stared out at the grey sky and thought, *Lloyd's right. We must stop the Headmaster. I've got to THINK.*

As she finished her drink and walked back to Intensive Care, she ran over everything SPLAT had discovered so far, trying to fit the pieces together. There was something hovering at the edge of her mind. Something she'd missed. If only she could work that out . . .

But she didn't manage it. Because as soon as she walked into Intensive Care, Bernadette gave a huge grin.

'It's all fixed. He's gone down to have the EEG now, and if the results are OK—and I'm sure they will be—the bandages are coming off at four o'clock.'

Dinah grinned back. And she forgot all about everything except the face under the bandages.

14

BEHIND THE MASK

Lloyd was speechless. He stared down at the man he had unmasked.

It wasn't the Headmaster.

This man was young—well under thirty—with a pale brown face and big dark eyes. He was gazing back at Lloyd with a cheerful grin, completely relaxed. He hadn't even taken his feet off the dressing table.

'We-ell,' he drawled. 'I never expected anyone to find me *here*. And I thought it would be the paparazzi who tracked me down in the end. But you're just a kid. You have *performed*.'

His voice was unmistakable—musical and growling at the same time. This was DJP all right. No one else could have imitated that sound.

The heavies were crowding into the room now, pulling at Lloyd's shoulders. DJP ordered them off with a flick of his hand.

'Don't you trouble this boy. He is a winner. Take your hands off him and make him *welcome*.'

The heavies drew back, but Lloyd barely noticed. He was still staring at DJP. Speechless.

DJP took his feet down and leaned forward. 'What's your problem? You don't like the way I look?'

'It's not—you're not—' Lloyd couldn't get the words out.

But Ingrid could. She came bursting through the door, pushing between two of the heavies. 'You're not him!' she said fiercely. 'You're not the Headmaster!'

DJP stared at her. 'You thought I was some kind of teacher? *Me?*'

Ian and Mandy edged into the room too, with Harvey sidling in behind them. DJP put up a hand jokingly, to hide his face from their stares.

'Hey there! You'll have me wanting my mask back. What's the story here? Do I look like I ought to be in school?'

'It's not what you look like,' Ian said. 'It's what you do—'

'You think I'm like a teacher because of what I *do*?' Without warning, DJP jumped to his feet, towering over them. He was a tall man and he was wearing high platform soles. The effect was startling.

'You think your headmaster moves like me? Hey?'

He strutted down the dressing room, turning dramatically at the end. 'You think a teacher can take a crowd of kids and hold their attention like this?' He stretched out a hand, palm upwards, and clenched it suddenly. 'Is this teacher of yours up with the latest music? Can he pick out a great new band, from the first play of its first track? Can he—'

'None of that,' Mandy said.

'So what is it?' DJP spread his arms wide.

Lloyd finally got his voice back. 'It's the people

you've met. They all say the same thing if anyone asks questions.'

'As if you'd hypnotized them,' said Harvey.

Ian chanted the sentence in a mechanical, robotic voice. 'I. Am. Not. Able. To. Give. Out. Any. More. Information. About. DJ. Pardoman.'

DJP stared for a second. Then he threw his head back and shouted with laughter. 'You think I *hypnotize* people? Man, that is soooooooooo cool.' He looked delighted.

Lloyd wasn't going to be tricked. 'If they're not hypnotized—why do they all say that?'

'Because—' DJP sat down and put his feet up again, beaming all over his face. 'Because it's in the *contract*, man. It was my manager's idea. They want me to visit? Then they have to keep my secrets. We write that line into the contract and my manager makes sure they're word perfect before he signs. And you thought—' He laughed again, pointing a finger at Lloyd.

'That's not the only thing,' Lloyd said sulkily. 'There's all that stuff about the bananas and the golden syrup. The way all the kids buy the same.'

DJP waved a hand dismissively. 'Don't pin that on me. That is ABSOLUTELY NOTHING TO DO WITH PURPLE. It's the kids who do it. By themselves.'

'Then there's the unmasking plan,' Mandy said gently. 'That's just the sort of thing the Headmaster would have done. To get everyone in the country looking into his eyes.'

DJP shook his head scornfully. 'Who'd want to

look into a *headmaster*'s eyes? I tell you—*I'm* the one everyone's wild to see.' He grinned. 'And you've found out more about me than anyone else has, so you get to do the unmasking!' He put his head on one side and studied them. 'All of you together? Or just the little girl on her own? She is soooooooo cute.' He ruffled Ingrid's hair.

One of the heavies appeared in the doorway with a tray.

'You need to get filming, DJP,' he said. 'Or they won't make the deadline. Can't the kids wait till you take a break?'

'Sure they can,' said DJP, without asking. He jumped up, waving a hand. 'Get their details. I'll be back in an hour.'

He was gone in a flash. The heavy put the tray down on the table. It was loaded with cans of drink and packets of nuts and crisps.

'No trouble now,' he said. He took a notebook out of his pocket. 'The manager's going to want all your details. Names and addresses and phone numbers.'

Ingrid took the notebook, frowning as she started to write. 'Have we got to hang around here for a whole hour? What are we supposed to do?'

The heavy shrugged. 'Do what you like. Talk to each other. Take a nap. Read the newspaper. No one's got time to entertain you.'

He stood looming over them while they all wrote down their details. Then he picked up the notebook and disappeared.

Ian looked round the room. 'It's not exactly amusing in here, is it? There isn't even a TV.'

'There are some books over there,' Mandy said.

She pointed at the shelf in the corner of the room. It was full of tall, thick books, bound in red and green leather. Their spines were blank, except for a single number in gold.

'They don't look very interesting,' Ingrid muttered.

'Better than nothing.' Lloyd went across to the shelf. He was curious to know what sort of reading DJP kept in his dressing room. Novels? History? Updates on the music industry? He lifted down one of the books and opened it.

Harvey looked over his shoulder and gasped. 'It's full of press cuttings!'

'Weird!' said Ingrid. She ran across to pull out the next one. And the next.

They were the same—full of press cuttings about DJP, arranged in chronological order. There were ten books altogether, going back to the very beginning of DJP's career, and every one was crammed with bits of newspaper. The first cuttings were stuck in carefully, but the later ones were just dabbed in, and they fluttered as the pages turned. Halfway through the last book, there was a bundle of cuttings still waiting to be added.

From every picture, the electronic mask stared out at them, showing improbable faces. Margaret Thatcher in London. The Pope in Scunthorpe. Pop stars in Edinburgh and Aberystwyth and footballers in Truro and Belfast.

'It's pathetic!' Ingrid said. 'Fancy collecting your own press cuttings like that!'

'Maybe he likes to remember all the people he's met,' Mandy said kindly.

'Like that weirdo Ingrid and I went to find?' Ian grabbed a book and began to leaf through it. He turned the pages so fast that a couple of cuttings fell out.

'Careful!' Harvey said anxiously.

Ian slipped the cuttings back into place and went on more slowly. 'Here she is. Only her hair's twice as long now. It's like talking to a haystack. And it's really electric. If you get too close, it goes up your nose.'

Mandy laughed. 'Not like our boy. He was very smart.' She flicked through and found a picture of a small boy with his hair slicked back.

'Ours was twice that size.' Lloyd opened the newest book, looking for a picture of Dennis. But he couldn't find one. 'I don't think he's here.'

'Maybe the cutting's not stuck in yet.' Mandy took out the bundle of loose pieces and unfolded it, spreading the cuttings across the dressing table. Some of them were trimmed ready to stick in, but some had just been torn out roughly. She began to turn them all the right way up and Lloyd leaned over, watching her.

'Stop!' he said suddenly.

'That's him?' Mandy put the bundle down and looked at the last cutting. There was Dennis Ryan, filling over half the picture as he grinned at DJP. 'Wow! He's huge!'

But Lloyd wasn't interested in Dennis any more. He had caught a glimpse of the other picture on that page.

Local author Phil Ashby proudly displays his new history of Great Ley. The caption was familiar—but the face was all wrong.

'What's up?' Harvey said. He leaned over to look at the photograph.

Mandy was watching Lloyd's face. 'Someone you know?' she said gently.

Lloyd's head was spinning. 'Dinah's gone to visit him. In hospital. She thinks he's her father.'

Ingrid wriggled past Mandy so that she could see. 'He doesn't look much like Dinah.'

'He doesn't look like her father, either,' Lloyd said. 'Not in this picture. But he did when Dinah found it on the internet! She found the same article with a photo just like this—except that the man in that one looked *exactly* like her father's photo.'

'The internet picture was different?' Ian said.

'Only the face.' Lloyd picked up the cutting and stared at it. 'This has got to be the real one, hasn't it? Someone altered the one on the internet.'

'But why?' Mandy said.

'I think it was planted there specially. For Dinah to find.' Lloyd worked it out as he spoke. 'Someone knew Dinah would be looking for stuff about DJP—and they set a trap.'

'Not much of a trap,' Harvey said. 'She must have spotted the difference as soon as she saw the real Phil Ashby.'

'But that's just it,' Lloyd said slowly. 'She hasn't seen him yet—because the man in hospital is covered in bandages. You can't see his face at all. They're taking the bandages off today—and Di's sitting beside his bed waiting for it to happen.'

That was it. That *had* to be it. But he couldn't see why anyone would go to all that trouble.

Ingrid looked indignant. 'What a mean trick! Just imagine how she's going to feel when he looks up at her and he isn't—'

Inside Lloyd's head, something flashed, like an electric spark. '*What did you say?*'

Ingrid looked startled. 'I just meant she'll feel terrible when he opens his eyes and looks up at her—'

'That's it!' Lloyd jumped up. 'We've got to get to the hospital! Dinah's in terrible danger!' He scooped up the cutting of Phil Ashby and headed for the door.

'Hang on,' Ian said. 'What are you talking about? Why is Dinah in danger?'

Lloyd couldn't believe they were being so slow-witted. 'Don't you get it? Who would *love* Dinah to stare into his eyes—so that he can get her in his power? Who's always trying to hypnotize her, so that he can use her brains?'

Mandy gasped. 'You mean—it's the *Headmaster* under those bandages?'

'It has to be!' Lloyd opened the door. 'Let's get out of here. We must reach the hospital before Dinah looks into his eyes!'

130

15

UNDER THE BANDAGES

When they brought Phil Ashby back from his EEG, Dinah was sitting waiting for him. The porters pushed his bed through the doors and down the ward to its place, and Dr Winthrop followed them.

When he reached Dinah, he looked down at her and nodded.

'You've done a good job with our patient,' he said. 'The test results are even better than I hoped. Now—are you brave enough to stay here and keep talking to him while we take off the bandages?'

'Of course,' Dinah said. 'I'll do anything that'll help.'

'All you need to do is talk,' said Dr Winthrop. 'And fix your whole attention on him. No need to worry about what the rest of us are doing.'

He glanced up at Bernadette, and she pulled the curtains round the bed, shutting out everything else. They were pale green curtains and the light filtered through them, taking on a strange, underwater quality.

Dinah leaned closer to the figure on the bed. 'It's me,' she said. 'Dinah. I hope you can hear me.'

The bandaged figure didn't move, but once again she had the feeling that, behind the bandages, his face was alert and attentive. Automatically, she looked for his hand to take hold of it. She was startled to see that it was wrapped in a loose white cotton mitten, with no thumb.

'It's so he doesn't scratch at his face,' Bernadette said, before she could ask. 'Wounds can be very itchy while they're healing.'

Dinah looked at the bandaged face again. 'Is he—very badly injured?'

'It was a serious accident,' Dr Winthrop said gravely. 'With any luck he won't be scarred too much, but he's going to look quite damaged until the stitches come out.'

Bernadette put a hand on Dinah's shoulder. 'Can you cope with that?'

Dinah nodded slowly. 'I'm just glad he's alive. And that he's getting better.'

She picked up Phil Ashby's hand, holding it in both her own. It felt surprisingly awkward—bigger and heavier than usual. For a moment, she almost wondered whether it was the same man under the bandages. Had they brought someone else back from the EEG?

But that was ridiculous. Pushing the thought to the back of her mind, she held the hand and began to talk in the steadiest voice she could manage.

'This is it, then. They're going to take off your bandages. Are you ready to open your eyes and see the light? It'll seem really bright, I expect, after all this time.'

While she was talking, Bernadette pumped at the handle on the far side of the bed, raising it to a convenient height for working. Then Dr Winthrop bent over Phil Ashby's head. He started snipping through the bandages, slitting carefully up one side until the whole front section was ready to lift away. Bernadette hovered at his elbow, ready to pass swabs or remove stray pieces of gauze.

All at once Dinah found it hard to breathe, but she forced herself to keep talking. Trying not to sound nervous. 'When they pull the curtains back, you'll be able to see the trees outside the window. It's a beautiful day. You've chosen a good time to wake up.'

The big hand in the white mitten lay loosely between her own hands, not moving. She couldn't feel any response at all.

Dr Winthrop snipped through the last piece of bandage. 'Ready?' he murmured.

Dinah nodded, and he began to lift the bandages away.

As he did so, the hand she was holding moved suddenly. The fingers closed round her fingers and tightened, gripping hard. Hurting. Automatically she tried to pull her hand free.

'Don't move!' Dr Winthrop said sharply.

Dinah bit her lip and kept still, fixing her eyes on the pad of bandages that was ready to lift away.

'Here we go, then!' Dr Winthrop lifted the last layer of gauze and whisked it off.

And Dinah found herself staring straight into the eyes underneath.

Huge, sea-green eyes.

And the face—

It was a face she knew. A familiar face. But seeing it there was so unexpected that her brain froze for a moment, refusing to work properly. *There aren't any scars*, she thought, ridiculously. *He doesn't look injured at all.*

And then she came to, with a jolt, realizing what had happened. It was a trap—and she'd walked straight into it. She was staring into the Headmaster's eyes.

For a split second, she waited for Dr Winthrop and Bernadette to ask what was going on. Then she understood that they'd already been hypnotized. Days ago. They weren't going to save her.

By then, it was too late to look away. The man on the bed had already begun to speak, talking in a steady, crooning voice.

' . . . *how tired you must feel after all that senseless emotion . . . feelings waste so much energy . . . you're very tired now, Dinah . . .* '

She had to stay awake! She had to work out what was going on! She struggled to turn her eyes away, but the Headmaster's eyes held her fast. He didn't need to grip her hand now. He didn't need anything except that cold, sea-green stare. And the voice that went on and on and on. Relentlessly.

' . . . *keep watching my face, Dinah . . . look at my face while I tell you what you see . . . next time you look at this face, your brain won't see me . . . your brain will tell you that you're looking at someone else . . . next time you look at me, you will see Stephen Glass . . .* '

The words washed over Dinah, on and on and on, until the darkness closed over her completely and everything dissolved . . .

When she woke up again, she wasn't next to the bed. She was sitting at the end of the ward, next to Bernadette's desk in the reception area. Bernadette was leaning over her, looking concerned, and the other two nurses were further down the ward, dealing with patients.

'What—what happened?' Dinah mumbled. She had no idea how long she had been sitting there.

'You passed out,' Bernadette said. 'Dr Winthrop took off the bandages and you keeled over.'

Dinah frowned, trying to remember. She had a very clear memory of Dr Winthrop cutting through the bandages over Phil Ashby's face. In her mind, she could hear every snip of the scissors. He'd cut through the bandages and asked her if she was ready. Then he'd lifted the bandages . . . he'd lifted them . . .

But it was useless. She couldn't remember anything after that.

'Don't worry about it,' Bernadette said briskly. 'Lots of people are squeamish. Can't stand the sight of blood and stitches and things.'

'But I'm not like that.' Dinah shook her head. 'Those things don't put me off.'

Bernadette shrugged. 'People often surprise themselves. And you must be very tired. You've been having an emotional time.'

*. . . how tired you must feel after all this emotion
. . .* Something stirred at the back of Dinah's memory, but she couldn't catch hold of it. It slid away like a wisp of smoke.

'What about him?' she said. 'What about Phil—about my father? Is he all right?'

'He's fine,' Bernadette said. 'Shall I take you down to see him now?'

For a second, Dinah hesitated. She didn't know why. She ought to have been desperate to go and see Phil Ashby without his bandages. But she felt . . . reluctant.

Before she could overcome the feeling, there was a sudden loud buzz from the double doors opposite the desk.

Bernadette looked annoyed. 'This isn't really a good time for visitors. Wait here a minute, Dinah, while I get rid of them.'

She stood up and went to the doors, opening them just wide enough to speak to whoever was outside.

'I'm afraid I can't let you come in—'

But a loud voice from outside interrupted her. 'We've *got* to come in. We must see Dinah.'

Dinah sat up sharply, startled. That was Lloyd's voice. What was he doing here?

'We need to see her before the bandages come off!' said another voice.

And that was Harvey. Dinah shook her head. Lloyd and Harvey were both supposed to be in London, visiting MediaJam. What was going on?

Suddenly, Bernadette gave an outraged gasp. She staggered back from the double doors, as if she'd been pushed. And Lloyd and Harvey came clattering into the ward, with Ian and Mandy and Ingrid close behind them.

'You can't behave like this!' Bernadette hissed. 'This is a ward full of seriously ill patients. You must all leave NOW, or I'll call security!'

Out of the corner of her eye, Dinah glimpsed the other two nurses looking up the ward, to see what was happening. She jumped up and went towards Lloyd. 'What are you doing?' she muttered. 'You can't behave like that. There'll be trouble!'

'We only want to speak to you,' Lloyd said.

'It's *important*!' said Harvey.

'Can't it wait till I come out of here?' Dinah felt a twinge of annoyance. 'When I get home we can talk about DJP all night if you like.'

'This isn't about DJP,' Ian said. 'It's about Phil Ashby. Show her, Lloyd.'

Lloyd put a hand inside his jacket and pulled out a piece of paper. 'Look at this,' he said.

It was a newspaper cutting. Dinah took it and the first thing she saw was a big picture of DJ Pardoman. 'That *is* about DJP!' she said. Even more annoyed now.

'Not that bit,' Ingrid said. 'Look lower down.'

Dinah's eye flicked to the bottom of the page. She read the caption first. *Local author Phil Ashby proudly displays his new history of Great Ley.* And then she saw the picture. Phil Ashby's face.

'You see?' Lloyd said. 'That doesn't look like your father at all, does it?'

'This must be the real picture,' Mandy said gently. 'Someone must have altered the one on the internet.'

Dinah stared at the face in the photograph. 'I . . . I can't—' She didn't know what to say.

Ian was peering down the ward. 'Where is he, anyway? When are they going to take off the bandages?'

'They've done it already,' Dinah said.

'And?' said Ingrid impatiently.

'I didn't really see his face. I—' Dinah wanted to explain what had happened, but somehow she couldn't get the words out.

She was still struggling when Bernadette interrupted. 'I don't know what all this is about,' she said briskly. 'But it sounds as though a quick look at Mr Ashby would settle the whole silly business. I'll take you down to look at him—*if* you can be quiet and behave properly.'

'We'll be like mice,' Ingrid said. 'Like tiny little mice. We won't make a sound.' She pressed her lips together and smiled winningly up at Bernadette.

Bernadette didn't look impressed, but she led the way down the ward to the bed at the end. The green curtains were still pulled round it and she stopped outside and looked severely at them all.

'I mean it about being quiet,' she whispered. 'He's still very weak.'

'We'll be quiet,' Lloyd said. 'Don't worry.'

He glanced at Dinah, as though he expected her to say something, but she couldn't respond. All her attention was on the curtains—and the man behind them. *Had* she seen his face before she passed out? If so—what was it like? Why couldn't she remember?

Was it so horribly scarred and disfigured that her mind had blotted the whole thing out?

Bernadette put a finger to her lips and pulled back one of the curtains, holding it out of the way to let them all go through to the bedside. Dinah and Lloyd led the way.

And there he was. Phil Ashby. He was lying slightly propped up in bed, facing them. Dinah found herself staring at a bruised and battered face, crisscrossed by lines of stitches. The skin was stretched and swollen, pulling awkwardly at the stitches. The puffy eyelids flickered and she caught her breath as they opened.

His eyes stared straight at her.

And they were blue.

'It's not him!' Lloyd hissed, glancing round at the others.

It's not my father, Dinah thought.

A great, sick wave of disappointment rose up inside her mind. For a moment, she thought she was going to pass out all over again. The face that looked up at her was the one from Lloyd's newspaper cutting. The real Phil Ashby. Her father, Stephen Glass, was dead after all.

The man's eyes focused with an effort, fixing on her face. And his fingers shifted slightly on the bed.

'Look,' Bernadette said, from over Dinah's shoulder. 'He wants you to take his hand.'

Out of the blue, Dinah felt a sudden, overwhelming surge of fear and revulsion. *I can't! I can't touch him!* Then she looked down at Phil Ashby's hand—and it was exactly the same as it had always been. Square and tanned, with strong, blunt fingers. *It's all right*, she thought. *It's really him.*

And then she was cross with herself. Of course it was him. How could it be anyone else? Slowly, she reached out and took his hand. It closed lightly round hers, with the familiar, weak squeeze, and once again she had a sense of being specially linked to him.

Phil Ashby wasn't her father—but they were still connected. Because he had responded to her voice when he was unconscious. Dinah smiled down at him and his mouth moved feebly, smiling back. Then his eyes closed and he fell asleep again.

'Is he going to be all right?' Mandy said softly.

'He's going to be fine,' said Bernadette. 'Thanks to Dinah. But he needs to rest now.'

She began to usher them all away from the bed. Dinah lingered behind for a moment, looking down at the sleeping figure on the bed. *I'll come and see you again*, she thought. *Very soon.*

Then she followed the others out of the ward.

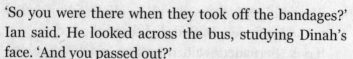

'So you were there when they took off the bandages?' Ian said. He looked across the bus, studying Dinah's face. 'And you passed out?'

Dinah nodded. 'That's what Bernadette said. I was

out for quite a while, I think. Bernadette thought it was because of all the scars and stitches and everything.'

'They weren't that bad,' said Harvey. 'Not bad enough to make anyone faint.'

'Maybe I was just . . . disappointed.' Dinah looked out of the window, avoiding their eyes for a moment. 'I really did think he was my dad, you know.'

'I wish I knew who faked that photograph!' Ingrid said hotly. 'It was a horrible, cruel thing to do. If I ever get hold of the person who thought of it, I'll . . . I'll . . . I'll *discombobulate* him!'

'I don't want anyone discombobulated,' Dinah said. 'I just want to know *why*. What was the point of tricking me like that?'

'Maybe it was a coincidence,' said Lloyd. 'Perhaps someone hacked into the website and altered the picture for fun—using any old photo. And it just *happened* to be your dad's and you just *happened* to see it.'

Dinah pulled a face and shook her head. 'The odds against that would be about ten billion to one. Someone was trying to trick me all right. But *why*?'

'Maybe . . . they were trying to keep you out of the way,' Mandy said hesitantly. 'So you wouldn't find out too much about DJP. Maybe they put that photo there to distract you if you started doing research about him.'

'But . . . they still couldn't be certain I'd find the photo.' Dinah leaned her face against the window next to her, trying to puzzle the whole thing out. 'There must be thousands of sites on the internet that mention DJP.

Hundreds of thousands. How could anyone make sure I was going to see *that* one?'

There had to be a way to work it out. Somewhere along the line she'd missed a clue.

But what was it?

BUT . . . WHERE IS THE HEADMASTER?

When they reached the Hunters' house, Mrs Hunter met them at the door—looking relieved.

'Thank goodness!' she said. 'I thought you'd never get here!'

'What's up?' said Lloyd.

Mrs Hunter lowered her voice. 'Mandy's cousin's here. And she's brought some very strange people with her. They said they weren't going away until they'd seen you.'

Ellie? What did she want? Lloyd frowned.

'Let's go and talk to them,' said Mandy.

Lloyd nodded and led the way into the sitting-room.

Ellie was lounging on the couch, with her feet on the coffee table—and twelve other girls were draped round the room. They were all First Purples, looking exactly like Ellie. White faces. Black eyes. Purple lips. They were all dressed in old clothes, with lots of jewellery. And purple phones clipped to their belts.

When the door opened, they lifted their heads and stared. And Dinah caught her breath.

'We've been waiting for you,' Ellie said.

She snapped her fingers and one of the other

girls turned round to the computer. It was already running and she got rid of the screensaver with a quick movement of the mouse. Suddenly the whole screen glittered purple and silver, with lime-green words spinning lazily across it.

INGRID   LLOYD
MANDY   HARVEY   IAN

'It's us!' Ingrid said.

'But what are our names doing there?' said Harvey. 'What is it?'

'It's DJP's website.' Ellie snapped her fingers again and the girl by the computer clicked on one of the names. They all dissolved and a line of text began to scroll continuously across the screen.

SEE THE UNMASKING WEDNESDAY 10 PM
AT PURPLE AND ON TV SEE THE
UNMASKING WED

'You've cut me out.' Ellie's voice was cold. 'You promised to tell me what you discovered—but you didn't. You went off and found DJP on your own—and now you're going to the unmasking without me.'

'I'm sorry,' Mandy said. 'It sort of happened by accident.'

'I don't like accidents,' Ellie said icily. 'What are you going to do about it?'

Dinah had been very still, ever since they all walked

into the room. Suddenly she said, 'Who told you, Ellie? Who told you we found DJP?'

Ellie's eyes went suddenly blank. 'Nobody told me,' she said. 'I just knew.'

Dinah gave a small, thoughtful nod. Lloyd wondered what she was thinking.

She didn't explain. She just asked another question. 'You know the first time we came to Purple, Ellie? Who told you we had to bring bananas?'

Ellie's eyes didn't flicker. 'Nobody told me. I just knew.'

Lloyd felt the little hairs prickle at the back of his neck. He knew what was going on now. He knew exactly what Dinah was thinking.

Dinah didn't make any comment. She looked at the girl sitting next to Ellie. 'How about you?' she said. 'Who told you to take golden syrup last week?'

'Nobody told me,' the girl said automatically. 'I just knew.'

'And this week?' Dinah glanced over at the girl by the computer. 'Who told you about the eggs?'

For the third time, the answer came back, exactly the same. 'Nobody told me. I just knew.'

Lloyd's brain was racing. They'd all been hypnotized! All those First Purples who'd gone to the opening of the club. Someone was using them to spread messages to the other kids.

That stuff about bananas and golden syrup didn't seem very important—but it was a crucial part of the plan. Without the shortages, most adults would have ignored DJP. But the shortages had made them furious—and they'd be watching the unmasking too, itching to see his face.

Ellie didn't like Dinah's questions. 'Why don't you stop wasting time?' she said. 'I don't want to talk about golden syrup. I want to talk about the unmasking.'

The other Purples all nodded, staring coldly.

Lloyd tried not to shudder. 'What do you want?' he said. 'We can't do anything about it now.'

Ellie looked him up and down. 'You can give me one of the invitations,' she said. 'I'll go instead of Mandy.'

'But that's not fair!' Ingrid burst out. 'Mandy's done more than anyone. She *deserves* to go.'

Ellie didn't say anything. She just looked round at all the other First Purples. Then she stared at Mandy. Waiting.

But it was Dinah who spoke. 'How about it, Mandy?' she said.

Lloyd was amazed. What was she up to?

Mandy was obviously startled too, but she didn't say so. She looked steadily at Dinah for a moment. And then she nodded. 'Yes, you can have my place, Ellie. No one's going to know the difference.'

Ellie gave a small, satisfied smile. 'That's all right then,' she said. 'We can all go together, can't we? You and me, Lloyd, and Ian and Harvey and Ingrid.'

She stood up suddenly and the other girls copied her. Without bothering to say goodbye, they all swept out of the room, leaving the door open behind them. Lloyd heard his mother's voice in the hall.

'You're off now? Well, thanks for coming and I hope—oh!'

The front door slammed before she could finish speaking.

Lloyd stood up and closed the sitting-room door. Then he looked at Dinah. 'What was all that about?' he said. 'You let her get away with it.'

'We need to know where she is,' Dinah said. 'To keep an eye on her. Don't you realize how dangerous she is?'

'Dangerous?' said Harvey. 'What do you mean?'

Dinah looked down. 'I've remembered now how I found that photo on the internet. It was Ellie who put me on to the site.'

Of course! Suddenly Ellie's voice came back to Lloyd. *Don't waste time on all the national things*, she'd said, when Dinah began the search. *Try the local papers . . . I can tell you where he's been.* She'd even written a list of places.

'She's a spy,' Dinah said. 'She's been spying on us all the time.'

'But she doesn't know we've guessed,' Ian said slowly. 'So if *we* watch *her*—we might find out who's giving her orders.'

'She'll lead us to the Headmaster!' Ingrid was triumphant.

'If it really is him,' said Lloyd cautiously. 'We haven't got any proof.'

Ingrid was scornful. 'Of course it's the Headmaster! Who else would hypnotize people and set up a television unmasking that everyone's going to watch? It's him all right. And if we don't stop him, he'll be taking over the whole country on Wednesday evening.'

'But—where is he?' Mandy said.

There was an uncomfortable silence. Lloyd felt a huge wave of panic looming over him. He liked to have clear plans, to know the enemy he was struggling against. But this—it was like fighting a puff of smoke.

It was Dinah who broke the silence. 'We have to do the best we can,' she said. 'And we've got two chances. If you four go off with Ellie, you'll be able to watch her. *And* you'll be up on the stage, where everything's happening. One of those ought to lead you to the Headmaster.'

'What about you and Mandy?' Lloyd said.

Dinah took a deep breath. 'We'll be down in the audience,' she said. 'So we'll be able to move about freely. I think we ought to try and sabotage the television cameras.'

'WHAT?' Mandy looked horrified.

But Lloyd nodded gravely. 'Dinah's right. You'll have to try and smash the glass or cut off the electricity or something. You'll get into trouble, but that's just too bad. We've got to stop him somehow.'

The invitations to the unmasking arrived next morning, before school. They came by special delivery and Mrs Hunter brought the envelopes into the kitchen and watched while Lloyd and Harvey opened them.

'What's it all about?' she said. 'Isn't there one for Dinah?'

'We won a competition,' said Harvey. 'With Ian and Ingrid. But Dinah wasn't there.'

Mrs Hunter peered at the invitations. 'So you're going to that unmasking?'

'We're not just going,' Lloyd said. 'We're doing the unmasking.'

'Well done!' Mrs Hunter looked delighted. 'That man's ruining the country with silly games. I've been longing to see what's behind his stupid mask!'

'But you mustn't look!' Harvey said. 'You mustn't watch the unmasking!'

'Don't be silly.' Mrs Hunter laughed. 'Of course I'm going to look! I wouldn't miss seeing you on television. And anyway, everyone's going to watch it!'

No! Lloyd wanted to yell at her. *They mustn't watch! YOU mustn't watch!*

He wanted to yell it—but he knew she wouldn't listen. Whatever his mother and her friends did, there would be millions of people watching. And the Headmaster wasn't going to be defeated by getting a few people to turn off the News.

Mrs Hunter was smiling at Dinah. 'What about you? Are you going to stay here and watch with Dad and me?'

Dinah shook her head. 'I'm going with Mandy. We want to be in the club.'

'I suppose you do.' Mrs Hunter smiled. 'There'll be much more atmosphere there, won't there?'

There certainly will, Lloyd thought.

They had a final SPLAT meeting in the shed on Tuesday evening, to run over all the details. Lloyd was hoping that Dinah would have worked out where the Headmaster was by then. But she hadn't.

'We've just got to keep our eyes open,' she said. 'And be ready for anything.'

Harvey was looking very nervous. 'But suppose we're not fast enough? Suppose we get it wrong? Suppose—?'

'Stop supposing!' Ingrid said. 'You'll just make us all feel dreadful.'

Harvey looked even paler. 'But—'

'Don't worry.' Dinah put an arm round his shoulders. 'We may not be very strong or very fast, but there's one thing we've got that the Headmaster's never going to have. Not in a million years.'

Ian raised an eyebrow. 'And what's that?'

'It's SPLAT,' Dinah said. 'We've got each other. And every one of us is committed to defeating the Headmaster.'

She stood up and held out one hand, speaking the first half of their password.

'The man who can keep order can rule the world.'

Before she'd finished, the others were on their feet, gripping her hand with theirs. They all said the second half of the password together.

'But the man who can bear disorder is truly free.'

'We're going to win,' Dinah said. 'Because we've got to.'

BACKSTAGE

On Wednesday morning, Dinah and Mandy started out for school as usual, with the others. But they hadn't gone far before they realized that there was something wrong. Normally the streets were crowded with people their age, but today—there was hardly anyone around.

'I bet they're all at Purple already,' Ian said. 'Queuing for tonight.'

Dinah frowned. 'I ought to have guessed. I was planning to go straight after school, but that won't be soon enough, will it? We'd better go now.'

Mandy pulled a face, but she nodded. 'We'll never get in otherwise.'

'You mean you're going to spend the whole day in the car park?' Ingrid was appalled. 'You'll get freezing cold. And what are you going to *eat*?'

'We'll have to buy something,' Dinah said. 'Or we won't be able to think straight by tonight. The unmasking's not until ten o'clock.'

They all turned out their pockets and scraped together enough to buy some apples and rolls and four small bottles of water.

'What about eggs?' Ingrid said. 'You've got to have eggs, for the end.'

'I brought some from home,' Dinah said. 'I knew we wouldn't be able to buy any on the way.' She lifted the box out of her backpack and stowed everything else underneath. Then Lloyd and Harvey went into school with Ingrid and Ian—and she and Mandy caught the next bus out to Purple.

When the bus pulled up, outside the supermarket, they could already hear the crowd chanting in the car park behind.

'We want to **SEE**

D—J—**P**!

We want to **SEE**

D—J—**P**!

HIS **FACE!** HIS **FACE!** HIS **FACE!**'

There was a violent edge to the voices. Mandy shuddered as she and Dinah stepped off the bus and walked round to the back of the supermarket.

'They sound really worked up. And they're going to be much worse by this evening. The ones who get shut out will go crazy.'

'No they won't,' Dinah said. 'They'll be too busy watching the show. Look.' She pointed across the car park.

On the front of the club, high above the silver shutter, a huge screen had been put up, covering the letters that spelt out P-U-R-P-L-E. It stretched from side to side of the building.

'He's thought of everything, hasn't he?' Mandy said unhappily. 'And we haven't really got a plan at all. Dinah—do you think he's going to beat us this time?'

'No I don't!' Dinah said firmly. She wasn't going to tell Mandy how worried she was. 'We're SPLAT. Remember? And we're committed to defeating him. Come on. Let's try and get nearer the front.'

Quietly, the two of them joined the crowd. Without drawing attention to themselves, they started to move forward, inch by inch, slipping unobtrusively into every little gap that opened up.

They kept their heads down and talked in very low voices, and gradually they got nearer to the silver shutter. But it was hot work and they were tense all the time. After half an hour, Mandy tapped Dinah on the shoulder.

'Can I have some water?'

'Good idea.' Dinah took two little bottles out of her bag. She handed one to Mandy and opened the other herself. And she lifted her head to drink.

That was a mistake.

They were standing close to one of the white-faced girls—and the movement caught her eye. She glanced round and when she saw Dinah she started yelling.

'It's her! It's the one he told us to watch out for!'

She reached for her phone and half a dozen of the other girls crowded round, seizing Dinah and separating her from Mandy.

'What's going on?' Dinah shouted. '*Who* told you to watch out for me?'

The moment she'd asked the questions, she knew what the answer was going to be. The girls all said it at once, bellowing the words above the noise of the crowd.

'NOBODY TOLD ME! I JUST KNEW!'

Mandy pulled at the girls' shoulders, trying to get through to Dinah, but it was no use. They jabbed at her with their elbows, shoving her out of the way.

Dinah was trying to reach out to her when the crowd parted suddenly. Two of the heavies from the club came striding through. Marching up to Dinah, they caught hold of her arms, wrenching her free of all the other clutching hands. Without a word, they lifted her off her feet.

'Hey!' Mandy yelled. 'You can't do that! Leave her alone!'

The heavies ignored her. They turned round and began to carry Dinah away through the crowd.

'Dinah!' Mandy yelled. '*Dinah!*'

She struggled to follow, but the white-faced girls crowded back, blocking her way and shutting her in. Dinah could see it was pointless for her to fight them.

Twisting her head round, she shouted, 'Don't worry about me! Just stay here and make sure you get into the club!'

'I'll tell the others!' Mandy called.

She took out her own phone—but the girls just pulled it out of her hand and tossed it away. That was the last Dinah saw of her, because the heavies had reached the front of the club and they swung left, going down the side of the building.

There was a small door at the rear of the side wall. As they approached, it opened and, without breaking stride, they marched in, carrying Dinah with them. She found herself backstage, in a bare, white corridor that stretched from one side of the building to the other. On the right, two plain wooden doors led through into the club. On the left, there were half a dozen little dressing rooms and offices.

The heavies carried her right down the corridor, to the far end. The last door was slightly ajar and they stopped outside it.

'We've got the girl,' one of them called.

Without a sound, the door swung open. Dinah had a glimpse of a windowless office with ugly furniture and a hard floor. The walls were bare except for a security camera high up near the ceiling.

Before she could catch her breath, the heavies dropped her, so suddenly that she almost fell over. Planting a hand in the middle of her back, one of them shoved her into the room. She went staggering through the door, unable to stop herself.

'You can't keep me here!' she yelled. 'Let me go!'

She hit the desk and spun round, ready to race out of the room. But a man stepped out from behind the door and slammed it shut, standing in front of it to block the way out. His eyes were hidden by dark glasses, but Dinah knew who he was. Behind those dark glasses was the face that she feared most in the whole world.

The cold, pale face of the Headmaster.

Dinah was terrified—but she knew that she had to seize this chance. If she let the Headmaster stare into her eyes, she would be hypnotized and helpless. But while he was wearing dark glasses, she was safe—and she had to *use* that time, to discover what he was plotting.

She took a step forward. 'What are you doing?' she said. 'Why have you brought me here?'

The Headmaster's mouth twisted into a thin, satisfied smile. 'I wanted to tell you that you and your friends have failed. This time, you are not going to ruin my plans.'

'You haven't succeeded yet!' Dinah said defiantly.

The Headmaster's smile didn't waver. 'But I will. And you are going to help me, Dinah. That will be my crowning triumph. You are going to betray your friends and help me to take control of the country.'

'You're mad!' Dinah said fiercely. 'I'll never help you! Never!'

'Oh, but you will.' The smile vanished suddenly and the Headmaster's voice was as cold as steel. 'I have analysed all our past meetings to learn from what happened. And this time I know how to make my plans succeed. It isn't enough to defeat the forces of disruption and chaos. They must be humiliated and demoralized. And that is what will happen to you and your pathetic friends.'

Dinah was trembling, but she kept her voice steady. 'It doesn't matter what you do! I'm not going to help you—*and your plans aren't going to succeed!*'

'You still think you can defeat me?' The Headmaster sounded amused now. 'Don't you realize that you have been my puppets, all along? I knew that you and your friends would try to interfere with my plans—so this time I channelled your interference. I deliberately fed you information—and arranged to have you watched, every step of the way.'

'You didn't fool us!' Dinah said. 'We know all about Ellie and the First Purples. We know they're your spies!' She didn't say how long they'd taken to find out.

'And what about my plan to keep *you* out of the way?' The Headmaster's smile was thinner and sharper now. 'Don't pretend that you guessed that too. I had you completely fooled, Miss Clever Dinah Hunter. You couldn't tear yourself away from your *father*'s bedside.'

'Phil Ashby *isn't* my father!' Dinah snapped.

'Of course he isn't. But does that really matter?' The Headmaster's voice was scornful. 'What's the difference? A few genes? How can an intelligent girl like you be influenced by something so primitive?'

'It has to do with feelings,' Dinah said.

'Feelings?' A look of disgust flickered across the Headmaster's face. 'Feelings are useless and wasteful. They create chaos and destroy order. This country will never be run efficiently until *feelings* are abolished.'

'You can't do that!' Dinah said. But she remembered Ellie and the other First Purples, with their blank, emotionless faces, and she knew that he could.

'I *can* do it—and I *will*!' The Headmaster's voice rose in triumph. 'By midnight tonight, this country will be swept clean of feelings. I shall set people free from fear! From jealousy! From anger and pain and hatred!'

'What about happiness?' said Dinah. 'What about

excitement and sympathy and delight? What about love? Are you going to get rid of those too?'

'Naturally,' the Headmaster said. 'I shall abolish all that degrading, sentimental rubbish. People's lives will be calm and efficient—and simple.'

'But they'll be dead inside!'

'And is that so bad?' The Headmaster dropped his voice suddenly. 'Think how feelings drag you down. Remember what you went through in the hospital, Dinah. Wouldn't you like to use your brains without being distracted like that? Wouldn't you like a life that's as pure and straightforward as mathematics?'

'I—' Dinah wanted to fling the words back at him. To shout, *No! I don't want that!* But the turmoil of the last few days surged up inside her head and, for a split second, she hesitated.

In that second, the Headmaster reached up suddenly and pulled off his dark glasses.

Now! Dinah thought. *Now I must close my eyes. Now—*

But she couldn't. Because—in the split second when it would have been possible—she glimpsed the face behind the dark glasses. And she saw something quite different from what she was expecting. Quite different from the Headmaster's long face with its waxy, paper-white skin and pallid lips.

She found herself staring at a young man with dark brown eyes, crinkled slightly at the corners. They were friendly, smiling eyes and his mouth was smiling too as he reached out a hand towards her.

'Hello, Dinah,' he said. 'Don't you recognize me? Don't you know who I am?'

There was something not quite right about the voice, but she couldn't take that in, because her whole attention was concentrated on the face. The face that she knew so well—even though she couldn't remember seeing it.

The mouth smiled again. She knew the shape of those lips as well as she knew her own—but she had never thought that she would see them moving.

'Who am I?' they said. 'Say my name, Dinah. Speak it out loud.'

It's impossible, said Dinah's brain. *You mustn't believe it. You mustn't be taken in.* But how could you disbelieve the evidence of your own eyes? Those brown eyes smiled at her and the mouth spoke—and she found her own mouth shaping words she had never thought she would speak.

'You . . . you look like Stephen Glass,' she said. Stammering slightly because of the sheer weight of her feelings. 'You look like my father. But you can't be—'

His smile was so delightful that she couldn't tear her eyes away from it. Not even when his voice began to croon at her.

'Trust me, Dinah, trust me . . . it's hard to take in, but you can trust me . . . I can see you're very tired, but don't be afraid . . . all you need is a little sleep . . . and then I'll tell you what we're going to do . . . '

'I mustn't sleep,' Dinah mumbled. 'I've got to understand what's going on . . . I've got to work it out . . . '

But her tongue was thick in her mouth, stumbling over the words. She fought to keep her eyes open, but her eyelids had started to get heavy. And the voice crooned on and on.

' . . . *trust me, Dinah, trust me . . . there's no one closer than your own flesh and blood . . . no one at all . . .* '

She had to stay awake. She had to stay—

But she couldn't. She was sinking into the depths of a vast, dark sea. Falling down, down, down into a place where there was no speaking or thinking or feeling. Down and down and down . . .

ON CAMERA

Ellie was round at the Hunters' house by half past five, waiting to set off for the unmasking. Ian and Ingrid arrived just after eight. But it was almost nine o'clock before the car came to collect them.

It was a big purple limousine, driven by a chauffeur in a purple uniform. He opened the passenger door and stood to attention while the five of them trooped out of the house and into the car.

'Have a good time!' Mrs Hunter called, waving them off. 'And get that mask off! Remember—I'll be watching you!'

'No, don't,' Harvey muttered under his breath. 'Please don't.'

Lloyd gave his ankle a warning kick. *Shut up, you idiot*, he mouthed. Ellie was sitting opposite them, her eyes darting everywhere. They couldn't afford to give anything away.

When they reached Purple, the limousine had to slow right down to edge its way across the car park. The session in the club had started, but there were a couple of thousand people standing outside, shut out. Hands thumped the limousine as they went through, and voices yelled all round them.

'We want to **SEE**
D—J—**P!**
His **FACE!** His **FACE!** His **FACE!**'

'They can't get into the car, can they?' Harvey said nervously.

'Of course not,' said Lloyd. But he was tense too. He hoped it wouldn't be too long before they were inside.

The limousine crawled round to the left side of the building and pulled up tight against a small door. The driver moved the glass partition and turned round to speak.

'Get inside fast,' he said. 'Before the kids work out a way of squeezing past the car. I'll be back to pick you up when it's all over.'

He hooted and the door of the building opened suddenly, inwards—making a space for Lloyd to open the side door of the limousine.

'Let's go!' said Ellie.

She shot out of the car and into the building, ahead of everyone else. As she went, Ingrid pulled a face behind her back.

'It's not the same with her here. I wish we had Dinah and Mandy instead.'

'They've got more important things to do,' said Ian. He went next, ducking out of the car straight into the club.

Lloyd gave Harvey a nudge. 'Go on!'

The crowd had closed round the limousine now and it was beginning to rock. Harvey scuttled out and Ingrid followed him, pushing at his back to make him hurry. Lloyd went last, slamming the car door shut behind him and scrambling into the building.

As soon as he was safely in, one of the heavies inside shut the door of the club and locked it. Catching his breath, Lloyd looked round.

He was expecting smart offices and luxurious dressing rooms, but there was nothing like that in sight. They were standing in an uncarpeted corridor behind the club itself. To the left, half a dozen doors opened off the corridor, but on the right there was only one, at the far end. It obviously led straight on to the stage. He could hear the thudding of the loudspeakers and the musical growl of DJP's voice.

'And now here's the new Number One—and it's the *best*!'

The music was so loud that Lloyd felt the floor of the corridor vibrate. But that sound was more than matched by the roar of voices, from all round. People were shouting—inside the club and out in the car park— and they were all yelling the same thing.

'We want to **SEE**

D—J—**P!**'

A brisk young woman with a clipboard came bustling down the corridor towards Lloyd and the others.

'Hi,' she said 'I'm Caroline. I'm a production assistant with the TV company and I'll be taking care of you this evening.'

'Great!' said Ellie. 'I can't wait for the unmasking!'

Caroline beamed. 'It's the biggest thing I've ever

worked on. We're putting the show out live on satellite to all the other clubs. DJP's manager reckons there'll be two million people watching—and another twenty-five million tuning in to the actual unmasking, on the News. Isn't that brilliant?'

Lloyd forced himself to smile, but it was a very weak smile. He was starting to feel desperate. There were dozens of people milling around backstage—technicians and heavies and assistants like Caroline. He'd been hoping for a chance to sneak off and investigate, but that was obviously impossible.

He and Harvey and Ian and Ingrid were all helpless, caught up in the television production. He just hoped Dinah and Mandy were doing better. Had they worked out how to disconnect the television cameras?

'You're going to need a bit of make-up,' Caroline was saying. She opened one of the doors on the left and hustled them into an office. 'Richard and Laura here will take care of that. I'll be back to fetch you in half an hour or so.'

'Make-up?' Harvey said. He looked at the mirrors and the boxes of cosmetics and pulled a face. 'Do we really have to?'

Ingrid gave him a push. 'Why not? Don't *fuss*.'

She was right, Lloyd thought gloomily. What did a bit of make-up matter? They could paint his face with orange flowers and purple jellyfish if that would help to defeat the Headmaster.

But it wouldn't help.

And he couldn't think of anything that would.

Half an hour later, he still hadn't thought of anything. And he'd run out of time. Caroline came bustling back into the room.

'OK, everyone. It's ten to ten. We need to get you on stage.'

She shepherded them out of the office and down the corridor to the door that led through to the stage.

'Here we go!' she said.

The body of the club was as dark as usual, but onstage it was hot and very, very bright. Lloyd could see one television camera on the far side of the stage and another out in the middle of the dancers, protected by barriers.

As they stepped into the light, DJP raised a hand in greeting. He came prancing across the stage towards them, with Charlie Chaplin's face on the front of his mask.

Was it *really* DJP? Or was it—the Headmaster? For a moment Lloyd hoped, wildly, that it was. If the Headmaster had taken DJP's place, then they would know what was going on. And he could start to make a plan.

But then DJP spoke—and Lloyd knew he was wrong. The face on the mask might change, but that voice was unmistakable.

'We-ell, hi to you all!' DJP said. 'Give them a cheer, everyone! These are five *great* detectives from the Purple audience!'

The crowd stamped and roared. Ellie waved back and Lloyd and the others copied her. Very half-heartedly.

DJP shook his head at them. 'Come on now! You've just been cheered by twenty-seven million people. Show a bit of enthusiasm! Are you ready for the unmasking?'

'No!' Lloyd said desperately. 'We're not! You've got to wait—'

'Wait?' DJP threw back his head and laughed. 'Television doesn't wait for anyone. They're going to connect up to the News at any moment. We're just standing by for the signal.'

He looked to the side of the stage and Caroline called from the doorway.

'Five seconds to go. You can start moving now.'

DJP waved a hand and walked to the front of the stage. Looking out over the audience, he raised a hand dramatically.

'It's NOW!' he shouted. 'It's . . . the unmasking!'

The music was cut off short. The dancing stopped abruptly. In the darkness, hundreds of pale faces looked up towards the stage. DJP spread his arms out.

'This is not my real face!' he said.

He lifted his head so that the mask faced straight into the television camera in the centre of the club. As he did so, the huge screen behind him lit up suddenly. The television picture of his mask appeared there, blown up to a gigantic size.

'This is not my real face!' DJP shouted again.

He turned towards Lloyd and the others, holding

out his hand as if he meant to call them over for the unmasking. But before he could speak, another voice interrupted, from the far side of the stage.

'And those are not the real unmaskers!'

A tall figure came striding on to the stage—a man with hair so pale that it was almost colourless and narrow, pallid lips. His long face was startlingly white under the lights and his eyes were hidden by dark glasses.

'It's the Headmaster!' screeched Ingrid. 'Run!'

But as she moved, the Headmaster stretched out one arm in a sudden, commanding movement, pointing across the stage. Immediately, a dozen heavies in purple tracksuits came pouring through the door behind Lloyd, cutting off that escape route.

'This way!' yelled Harvey, turning to jump off the stage.

He was moving quickly, but Ellie moved faster. The Headmaster pointed at her and she threw herself sideways flinging her whole weight against Harvey. He crashed into Lloyd and Ian, catching them both off balance, and the three of them tumbled to the floor. As they hit the ground, Ellie grabbed Ingrid's shoulders and pushed her over, on top of them.

Before they could recover, the heavies had surrounded them, standing shoulder to shoulder to make an unbreakable wall. They were looking inwards, and their faces were menacing.

'Make a sound—and you're in trouble!' one of them muttered.

'Those are not the real unmaskers!' the Headmaster

repeated in a loud voice. 'The right person is about to appear on stage. Are you ready?'

'Brilliant!' Caroline murmured from the wings. 'Fantastic reality television!'

DJP looked across at Lloyd and the others and shrugged elaborately. 'Sorry, guys. My manager has spoken. Tough luck.'

The manager! Lloyd thought. *Of course!* Now—when it was too late—the clues came leaping into his head. Things they should have spotted.

What had Ellie said, when they asked about her make-up? *I'm a First Purple. I was there on the opening night—when DJP was there himself, with his roadies and his manager* . . .

Dennis Ryan had mentioned the manager too, when Lloyd asked who drove the speedboat away. *Some man. His agent or his manager or something.*

And DJP himself had virtually spelt it out—if only they'd been listening properly. *It was my manager's idea . . . We write that line into the contract and my manager makes sure they're word perfect before he signs.*

They should have guessed where the Headmaster fitted in, long before they saw him. But they hadn't. And now it was too late and they were trapped. They were right up on stage, at the very heart of the unmasking—and they were completely helpless.

Mandy and Dinah were the only ones with a chance of stopping the Headmaster now. They couldn't prevent the unmasking, but they could still sabotage the television presentation. Lloyd peered down into the audience, trying to catch sight of them.

It was too dark to see anything much—but it didn't stay dark for long. The Headmaster stepped forward, into the very centre of the stage, with his dark glasses glinting. He pointed again—straight into the audience.

'The real winner is down there with you,' he said. 'It is time for the unmasking now—and the light will find the true unmasker.'

A single bright spotlight began to sweep over the upturned faces, circling round and round the club. Lloyd followed it with his eyes, but he wasn't waiting to see the unmasker. He was trying to catch a glimpse of Mandy and Dinah.

Round and round went the light, hovering and backtracking, hunting for one particular face. Lloyd craned his head sideways, peering between the shoulders of the heavies who shut him in. He bent and stretched and twisted to keep the patch of light in view.

And suddenly he saw Mandy!

She was only a few feet from the central camera, gazing up so that the light caught her full on. For a split second, Lloyd's heart jumped joyfully. She was there—in the right place! They could still beat the Headmaster!

Then he took in Mandy's hopeless, defeated expression. And, as the light circled slowly, he saw the people standing round her. She was hemmed in by ten or twelve girls—and every one of them had a white face and dark lips and black-rimmed eyes. The First Purples had her trapped. She was helpless too.

That just left Dinah. She was the only one who was still free. If they were going to stop the Headmaster, she would have to do it single-handed. Lloyd screwed up his eyes and clenched his fists, willing her to succeed. She had to stop him! She *had* to!

At that very instant, DJP gave a triumphant shout.

'And here she is! The real unmasker! The one who's going to make it all happen!'

Lloyd's eyes flew open—and there she was. In the full glare of the spotlight, a single figure was climbing out of the audience and up on to the stage. Without hesitating, without looking left or right, she walked up the steps and headed straight for DJP and his manager.

It was Dinah.

Like someone on parade, she marched up to DJP and shook both his hands. Then she turned to the Headmaster.

'She can't shake hands with *him*!' said Ingrid. She stood on tiptoe, peering between the heavies in front of her. 'Dinah!' she called. 'Dinah!'

Casually, Dinah looked round to see where the sound had come from—just as one of the heavies grabbed Ingrid and jammed a hand over her mouth. Dinah must have seen what happened, but she didn't show any reaction.

'She's looking straight through us!' Harvey whispered, in a voice that was shaking.

Dinah's eyes travelled over their faces in a detached, objective way, as if they were pieces of furniture.

Then, indifferently, she turned back to DJP and the Headmaster.

'He's done something to her,' Lloyd hissed. 'The Headmaster's hypnotized her—and now she's going to help him.'

'But she's still *herself*,' Harvey said. 'Even if she's hypnotized. He can't change that, can he?'

'Keep watching,' Ian said bitterly. 'It looks as though you're going to find out.'

The people in the audience were starting to get restless. Some of them were shuffling their feet and, away at the back, the chant was starting up again.

'We want to **SEE**

D—J—**P!**

We want to **SEE**

D—J—**P!**

HIS **FACE!** HIS **FACE!** HIS **FACE!**'

The Headmaster strode to the front of the stage and held up a hand.

'The moment has come,' he said coldly. 'The mask is about to be removed. You are going to see the face you have all been waiting for.'

He beckoned DJP forward and signed to Dinah to stand between the two of them. There was a fanfare of trumpets. And then—silence. For ten seconds, no one moved or spoke.

The tension in the club was almost unbearable. And beyond that club—in the other clubs, in all the homes where people were watching television—Lloyd knew that it would be exactly the same. Twenty-seven million people were waiting to see DJP's face.

The Headmaster spoke softly, into the silence. 'But which is the *right* face? Which is the face that everyone *really* wants to see uncovered?'

There was another pause. The whole country was holding its breath. Lloyd saw the heads in the audience turn as people looked from DJP, in his mask, to the Headmaster, in his dark glasses.

'What about you, Dinah?' The Headmaster's voice was very soft now, but his whisper was amplified to reach right to the back of the club. 'Which face do you want to see?'

Dinah's head turned too. Looking left and right and back again.

'It's your decision, Dinah,' the Headmaster murmured. 'Uncover the face you really want to see.'

For a split second, Dinah hesitated. Then she turned—

No! Lloyd thought. *No, she can't be doing that!*

MASKS AND FACES

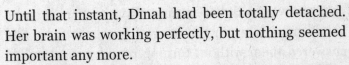

Until that instant, Dinah had been totally detached. Her brain was working perfectly, but nothing seemed important any more.

She knew who the manager was, of course, and what he wanted. But what did it matter if he took control of the country? And what did it matter that her friends were surrounded by heavies? She didn't feel a thing.

Nothing mattered. She was completely emotionless. Like a machine.

Then the Headmaster said, *Uncover the face you really want to see*—and, out of the blue, a wave of feeling hit her, like a hurricane. It was so strong that it almost knocked her off her feet.

The face you really want to see . . .

She knew what that was! It was the face that she had known only in a photograph. She had never expected to see it in real life—but if she took off those dark glasses, it would gaze back at her. She didn't know how she knew that, but it was fixed and certain in her head.

She *had* to see her father's face! The longing for that blotted out everything else. She didn't care about what was going on in the club, or about what the Headmaster would do if he got the chance. All she wanted was to see her father's smiling brown eyes and watch his mouth speak her name.

Ignoring DJP, she turned to the Headmaster and reached for his dark glasses. Dimly, she heard Ian and Harvey calling from the side of the stage.

'Dinah! Are you crazy?'

'Don't do it! You mustn't!'

Their voices didn't mean a thing to her, and she barely noticed when the heavies grabbed them. She answered them without turning round, as she pulled off the dark glasses.

'But it's my father! Look, it's my father's face . . . '

That's what she's seeing! Lloyd thought, in horror. He could hardly believe it, but her expression showed it was true. *When she stares at the Headmaster—she's seeing her father's face!*

And because of what she had done, everyone else was staring too. But they weren't staring directly at the Headmaster. They were looking beyond him, at the big screen. His face was there now, dominating the whole club. It was dominating all the other clubs too, and every television in the country. His sea-green eyes stared out at twenty-seven million people and his giant mouth began to whisper.

So the unmasking is over . . . you can see my face at last . . .

It was the end. He'd won.

Lloyd felt himself plunging down into a black pit

of despair. The Headmaster had finally beaten them—and he'd proved it by getting Dinah on his side. She'd betrayed her friends.

Lloyd wanted to stand and yell at her. He wanted to remind her about everything that the six of them had done together, all that they'd said and meant and fought for. But he knew it was hopeless. He wouldn't be able to get out more than a word before the heavies gagged him. And what could you say in a single word?

The Headmaster's gigantic face was still staring out at everyone. And his voice was crooning on and on.

. . . you must be feeling exhausted, so tired and sleepy . . .

Lloyd could hear the note of victory in his voice. Any minute now, he would have total control, and everything would be over. They might as well give in straight away. They were going to be defeated . . .

. . . so, so sleepy . . .

There was no chance—

But there was! Suddenly, Lloyd realized. There was only time to shout one word—but one word could be enough! There was one word that might bring Dinah back to herself. One word that summed up everything.

Flinging his head back, he yelled it at the top of his voice.

'SPLAT!' And again. 'SPLAT!'

One of the heavies lunged forward to grab him. But as his voice was choked into silence, Ingrid bit the hand that was jammed over her mouth. She twisted free and managed to shout the word a third time before she was gagged again.

'SPLAT!'

And from the audience Lloyd heard the thin sound of Mandy's voice, calling again and again as the First Purples tried to silence her.

'SPLAT! SPLAT! SPLAT!'

Dinah was growing drowsy as the Headmaster chanted. But she was fighting the drowsiness, because she wanted to go on looking at her father's face. And so she heard the shout coming from beside her and below.

'SPLAT!'

'SPLAT!'

The word exploded in her head. A hundred things that came jumping into her mind. She remembered the fun and the risks and the dangers they'd faced. She remembered their desperate struggles to defeat the Headmaster. She remembered everything.

But above all, she remembered the one thing that stayed the same through every test and every difficulty. *We're SPLAT—and we stick together.*

. . . your eyelids are growing heavy, crooned the Headmaster's voice from beside her.

Dinah took a long, slow breath.

She still had no feelings—except about her father. But her brain was working now. She didn't feel—but she knew. Whatever she felt like, she had chosen, long ago, to be a loyal member of SPLAT. And she'd chosen that because of what she believed. Because of what she thought was important. Her feelings might have changed but the world was still the same.

. . . your eyes are starting to close . . . crooned the Headmaster's voice.

Dinah thought about freedom and individuality and feelings—all the things the Headmaster wanted to abolish. SPLAT *had* to defeat him. They *had* to.

And suddenly she saw a way to do it!

In a single, quick movement, she turned to her right, reaching up for the mask that covered DJP's head. The face on the mask changed as she snatched at it, morphing from Queen Victoria into something flat and yellow. Dinah lifted the mask high and whirled round towards the Headmaster.

He turned slightly, to see what she was doing—and she met her father's face, full on. She took one last look at it, knowing that she would never see it again.

Then she pushed the mask on to the Headmaster's head, jamming it down so that it fitted tight. The picture on the big screen changed abruptly, to show the face on the mask.

Homer Simpson's face.

There was a split second of shocked, stunned silence.

Then everyone began to laugh. The heavies doubled up with laughter. Caroline gulped and gasped at the side of the stage. The First Purples shrieked hysterically. There was laughter inside the club. Laughter outside in the car park. Laughter in clubs and pubs and homes all across the country.

Twenty-seven million people were laughing uncontrollably.

Dinah heard the Headmaster bellowing with rage as he struggled to pull the mask off. His voice was unmistakable, but it came strangely from behind a shifting sequence of faces.

Charlie Chaplin and Bill Clinton and Madonna.

Frank Sinatra and Donald Duck.

The Prime Minister and an old woman with no teeth.

By the time he emerged, he was almost speechless with rage. He lunged towards Dinah with a roar. Lloyd pushed his way between the laughing heavies, with the others close behind him, and Mandy raced up on to the stage. They were heading for Dinah, to defend her from the Headmaster.

But they needn't have worried. When his real face finally reappeared, the crowd in the club didn't lose interest in him. Still laughing, they opened their backpacks and emptied out their pockets.

And they started throwing eggs.

Eggs hit the Headmaster's face, shattering into pieces. Egg white dripped off his hair and globs of yolk dropped down his cheeks and on to his chin. Bits of shell stuck to the side of his nose and trailed down the front of his clothes.

He looked ridiculous—and he looked a hundred times as bad on the big screen. It was almost sizzling with the anger that came sparking out of his eyes.

With a roar of fury, he turned on the six SPLAT members standing beside him.

'Once again, you have chosen chaos and disorder!' he bellowed. 'Once again, you have wrecked this country's chance of being run logically and efficiently. But don't think I'm going to give up! Don't think that your pathetic mockery—'

A whole egg hit him square in the mouth, cutting off the rest of what he was saying. Wiping the mess away, he flung Dinah a look of hatred and contempt. Then he stamped off the stage, to the sound of cheers from the audience.

DJP blinked for a moment, like someone coming out of a trance. Then he stepped forward, grinning cheerfully. 'Not sure what was going on there—but it must be time for another song!'

'Everyone thinks the whole thing was a joke,' said Mandy, in the SPLAT shed after school the next day. 'They don't realize what the Headmaster was up to.'

'Just as well,' said Lloyd. 'As long as they think he's a joke, he won't be able to do much.'

'He did look funny though, didn't he?' Ingrid said. 'He was so—so *eggy*!'

'Positively scrambled,' drawled Ian. He and Ingrid grinned, and Harvey and Mandy started to laugh.

Lloyd looked anxiously at Dinah, waiting to see if she joined in. Was she all right now? Or was she still . . . ?

Dinah stared back at him with empty eyes, not reacting. Her face was completely deadpan, not showing any expression. She looked utterly without feeling. Totally . . . totally—

She couldn't keep it up any longer. A huge grin spread across her face and she collapsed into laughter, pointing at Lloyd and gulping for breath.

'You thought . . . you thought—' She was laughing so much that she couldn't get the words out.

'You *weasel*!' Lloyd yelled. 'I thought you weren't OK. I thought—' He threw a cushion at her.

Dinah caught it neatly and sat on it with a grin. 'I'm fine,' she said. 'Everything's fine.'

Until the Headmaster tries again, she thought. But she didn't say it. She'd had enough of the Headmaster for the time being. There was something else she wanted to settle now.

'I'm going to see Phil Ashby on Saturday,' she said. 'I'd like to try and help him find out who he is. Does anyone want to come along?'

'We'll all come,' said Lloyd. He grinned at her. 'We stick together. Remember?'

'I remember,' Dinah said.

She raised a hand in the air and they all shouted, as loudly as they could.

'SPLAT!'

THE DEMON HEADMASTER IS BACK IN
A BRAND NEW ADVENTURE.

READ ON FOR A TASTE OF
WHAT'S TO COME IN . . .

'Good morning, Lizzie. Good morning, Tyler. It's an honour to welcome you to your first day at the *new* Hazelbrook Academy. The school where every student is a star.' The welcomer gave them a wide, friendly smile.

He looked like the perfect student. His face was scrubbed clean, his hair was slicked back, and his yellow tie was neatly knotted at the front of his gleaming white shirt. For a second, Lizzie almost didn't recognize him.

Then she felt Tyler shiver beside her. And she saw the bulldog face behind the smile. The broad, hefty shoulders and the brutal, heavy ridge of the welcomer's eyebrows.

It was *Blake*.

She shuddered, before she could stop herself, but Blake didn't seem to notice. He stepped back and waved a hand, ushering them through the doors. When they were inside, he made another little speech.

'As you can see, our school has been wonderfully transformed. You were unlucky to miss the induction on Day One of Hazelbrook Academy (where every student is a star). But Mrs Maron will see you now, to help you catch up with the rest of us.'

'Mrs Maron?' Lizzie frowned. 'Who's that?'

'Our new Deputy Head,' said Blake. 'Appointed by the Headmaster himself. Let me take you to her office.' He set off along the corridor, glancing back over his shoulder to make sure Lizzie and Tyler were following.

'Head*master*?' whispered Tyler.

That was different as well. What had happened to Miss Sefton, the old Head?

Blake led them past the hall and knocked on a door with a shiny new nameplate.

Mrs B. Maron—Deputy Head

They heard the sound of sharp high heels clicking across the room. The door flew open and a brisk, bright voice said, 'Lizzie, Tyler—good morning! I'm delighted to welcome you to the all-new Hazelbrook Academy.'

Mrs Maron was tall and elegant. Her smile was gleaming. Her neat blonde hair shone and her black shoes had heels like daggers. *Beata Maron: Deputy Head, Public Relations* said the badge on her smart yellow jacket.

She waved Lizzie and Tyler into her office. 'Wait there, Blake,' she said. 'I'll need you in a moment, to escort Lizzie and Tyler to the Headmaster's office.' She shut the door, marched across the room and looked down at her computer. 'Before you see the Headmaster, I need to update your records. We don't seem to have your parents' email addresses.'

'They haven't got a computer,' Lizzie said. 'Or a smartphones.'

'Not any more,' said Tyler. 'We had to spend all our money going to America, for Mum's—'

Mrs Marshall held up her hand to stop him talking. 'That is not acceptable. It's essential for parents to have access to the school website at all times. I'll have to sort something out.'

She gave a brisk nod and tapped at her computer keyboard. Then she marched back to the door and opened it. Blake was still outside, exactly where they'd left him, standing to attention.

'Take Lizzie and Tyler to the Headmaster's office,' Mrs Marshall said. 'Then return to your classroom and continue with your personal timetable.' She waved Lizzie and Tyler out of her room and shut the door smartly behind them.

'Please follow me,' Blake said. 'The Headmaster's office is this way.'

He started down the corridor and Lizzie and Tyler turned to follow him. But they had only taken a couple of steps when there was a strange whirring noise behind them. Looking over her shoulder, Lizzie saw a small yellow shape hovering in the air. It was high up, near the ceiling, and it had spindly black legs and a round, bright spot at the front—like a single, gleaming eye. For one horrible moment, she thought it was a giant insect.

Then it moved towards them, and she realized what she was looking at. 'It's a *machine*!' she said.

Blake glanced back and nodded. 'The Headmaster's eyes are everywhere,' he said.

'The Headmaster's *eyes*?' Tyler stared at him. 'What do you mean?'

Blake pointed up at the little yellow machine. 'Those are a key part of school security.' He recited the words as if he was reading them. 'They monitor behaviour and ensure that pupils are obedient and safe at all times.'

Lizzie shivered. 'You mean—they're spy drones?'

Just for a second, Blake's eyes flickered, as if she'd surprised him. Then he gave another of his polite smiles. 'Safety and security are essential to efficient learning,' he said, as he started down the corridor again.

Lizzie caught hold of Tyler's hand and gave it a squeeze. 'Maybe they'll keep you safe from *him*,' she whispered.

Blake stopped just ahead of them, outside a door that said *Headmaster*. Just at that moment, another boy came hurrying round the corner beyond him. He bumped into Blake, catching him off balance, and sent him staggering backwards. Blake crashed into the wall on the other side of the corridor, with a loud thud.

Oh no! Lizzie thought. *Now there's going to be trouble.* No one got away with pushing Blake around. Certainly not this boy. He was small and wiry—not much bigger than Tyler. He wouldn't stand a chance when Blake started on him.

But that didn't happen.

Blake blinked and stood up, straightening his tie. Then he looked apologetically at the strange boy. 'My fault for being in your way,' he said. 'Did I hurt you? Sorry, I don't know your name.'

'Ethan,' the boy mumbled. 'I'm Ethan—and I'm fine. It was my fault for not looking.'

'Don't worry about it,' Blake said politely. 'Do you need any help?'

The boy looked up and down the corridor. (Was he new? Lizzie was sure she'd never seen him before.) 'I'm supposed to be going to the changing rooms,' he muttered. 'But I don't know where they are.'

'Go down to the end of this corridor.' Blake pointed the way. 'Then turn left and straight on through the double doors. I'm sorry I can't take you there, but—'

'It's OK,' the boy said quickly. 'I know the way now.' He set off down the corridor.

'Go carefully,' Blake called after him.

Lizzie and Tyler looked at each other. What was going on? How come Blake was being kind and helpful? It was creepy. Lizzie kept waiting for him to change back to his old self and start thumping someone, but he just went on smiling. Was he—?

She never finished that thought. Because the door to the Headmaster's office swung open suddenly and a deep voice spoke from inside.

'Lizzie Warren and Tyler Warren, come in now.'

'Go on!' Blake gave them each a gentle push.

They stumbled through the doorway—into an empty room. There was a desk on the far side, with a single chair behind it, but no one was sitting at the desk. No one was anywhere to be seen. It was just a square, empty room, like a box.

Tyler edged closer to Lizzie, and she caught hold of his hand and squeezed it tightly. 'Don't worry,' she whispered. 'It'll be all right.'

'Silence!' said the deep voice they had heard before.

'I shall tell you if you are required to speak.'

The sound seemed to be coming from all around them. There had to be speakers somewhere, but Lizzie couldn't see them. It felt as if the room was talking.

'Lizzie Warren, you are a troublemaker,' said the voice.

'I'm not!' Lizzie said. 'I've never—'

'SILENCE!' The sound boomed through the empty air, almost deafening them. 'You are a troublemaker. Last term, you were almost excluded for fighting another student.'

'I had to do it!' Lizzie said fiercely. 'Blake kept bullying Tyler. I couldn't let him—'

The voice interrupted again and this time it was hard and cold. Like ice. 'Do not waste time making excuses. Stop talking and listen to me.'

Tyler started shaking and Lizzie put her arm round him.

Tyler didn't answer. He just turned very pale and pointed across the room.

The air next to the desk had suddenly started shimmering.

It was only a small patch at first, a tiny disturbance, so small it was hardly visible. But it began to spread, growing slowly larger and brighter. Thickening and changing colour. Gradually a shape formed in front of them, appearing out of thin air.

They found themselves looking at a tall man in dark glasses. He was dressed in black, from head to foot, but his hair and his skin were very pale, as though all the colour had been drained out of them.

Tyler gave a little, trembling gasp. 'What is it?' he whispered. 'Is he really here?'

'I think . . . it's a hologram,' Lizzie whispered back. She could hear her voice trembling too.

'You are not required to speak,' the man said sharply. 'You are useless troublemakers, with nothing valuable to say.' His eyes were still hidden, but his mouth curved into a small, tight smile. 'But you will not be useless for long. This school will turn you into useful members of society.' He lifted a hand to take off his glasses. 'Look at me. Both of you.'

Lizzie shivered. She didn't want to look, but before she could turn away the dark glasses came off—and she found herself staring into two green eyes like deep pools of water. Deep, deep . . .

No, she thought dizzily. *I won't look . . . He can't make me . . .*

But she didn't finish the thought. Her mind clouded over and everything dissolved in the depths of those cold green eyes. She was falling, falling, falling . . .

And then her mind went blank.